Memorial Day and Other Stories

Memorial Day and Other Stories

Paul Scott Malone

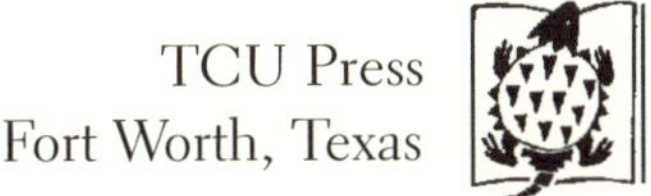

TCU Press
Fort Worth, Texas

Library of Congress Cataloging-in-Publication Data

Malone, Paul Scott.
Memorial day and other stories / Paul Scott Malone.
p. cm.
ISBN 0-87565-218-2 (cloth : alk paper—
ISBN 0-87565-219-0 (pbk :alk. paper)
1. United States—Social life and customs—20th century—Fiction. 2.
Young men—United States—Fiction. I. Title.
PS3563.A432464 M46 2000
813'.54–dc21 99-048286

Illustration and book design by
Barbara M. Whitehead

Acknowledgements

"Memorial Day, 1987: A Holiday Story" first appeared in the *Southern Humanities Review;* "When It's a House" in *Black Warrior Review;* "The Solitary Heart" in *Blue Mesa Review;* "Her Name Was Sheila Wells" in *Hawaii Pacific Review;* "Family Photos," Part I, in *The Tucson Weekly.*

For CK,
again and always,
and for Greg
and for Danny Frank
and for KJ

Also for
my mother
Lillian Annie (1924-1996)

Contents

Memorial Day, 1987: A Holiday Story

1.

Something's churning. Hardly slept last night and ever since I got up I've been racing around, looking for something, thinking thoughts so fast I've already burnt up a pack of Camels.

So now I'm in the attic scrounging for the flag. The Stars and Stripes. My Old Glory. Memorial Day is on Monday. Today is Saturday and we have no plans for the holiday but I'm as patriotic as the next guy and this year I want to show the flag. In a place called Flagstaff, Arizona, it ought to be a law.

Besides, we've had tragedy. As a nation, I mean: three dozen young sailors shot to pieces on an American warship in the Persian Gulf. A deadly mistake, says Brokaw, by the pilot of the Iraqi jet who fired the missiles; he thought he was killing Iranians. And on top of that an entire town in my home state of Texas was blown to Oz by a monster tornado. Children crushed. Grandmothers crippled. Twenty-nine dead. The TV shows incredible devastation, a flattened town on a flat desert prairie. In remembrance of fallen sailors, brave and true, and of dead Texans, old and new, I want to fly the flag.

I rip open a box marked MISC. On top are diplomas framed in wood and glass. Sarah's three are first, then my two—worthless now. I dig into the box. Here we go: red and white stripes wrapped around the multi-jointed pole. Digging deeper I find the string from which the flag hangs and the flagpole holder that you fix to the wall. But a part is missing. I keep scrounging. The flag was a gift from my dad when I returned from the war in '71. He had served in the Pacific during W.W. II, came home with only a stump for a left arm. Still on every holiday he flew the flag, the one the Army gave my grandmother after the funeral of my Uncle Bill. Uncle Bill died in Korea the month I was born.

Down below Sarah's making a racket with the vacuum cleaner. I call down through the hole in the ceiling, "Where'd we put the little knob?" and to my surprise the vacuum grinds to a stop. Some flagpoles have eagles; mine has a knob.

Sarah appears in the square hole. She's standing on the ladder. "What?" she snaps. I tell her what I'm searching for, and she offers up a look to match her tone. "A knob? I have no idea, William, I'd forgotten you even had a flag," she says and eases herself to the floor. Soon the vacuum starts up again.

We've been together for three years and two rent houses and I've never flown the flag in her presence. "That's not us," she says and she has a point. She's liberal; I'm agnostic. In all the years I've had it my flag has been outdoors only once—Independence Day, 1980, for the hostages in Iran. I was married then to a woman named Marge but that was our last July 4th together. My daughter Joy who is twelve will call tomorrow as she does on the Sunday of every holiday weekend, and that's on my mind too.

I give up on the knob and crawl downstairs. I take my hammer and some nails from the junk drawer in the kitchen and head out front. I hammer up the metal flagpole holder. I assemble the pole, unfurl and string up the flag. I turn, walk a few steps and turn again and it's then that I remember my dad always saluted the flag at this point. He would come to attention, the stump rigid against his rib cage, a Chesterfield hanging from his mouth, and he would snap his hand up to his brow looking as serious as if he were on the rocks of Iwo Jima.

None of my neighbors is out and Sarah couldn't see me where I am so I bring my hand up in a salute and then just as quickly make like I'm scratching an itch on my neck. And it's a good thing I was quick because here's Sarah coming around the corner of the house with Jocko. The dog prances up to me and sits. Then Sarah is with me. She slips her hand into the pocket of my jeans and the three of us stand there like an honor guard, motionless, staring at the flag as it whispers.

This is no way for a man to act. Sarah's at the grocery store, thank God, because I'm in front of the TV waiting for the Astros-Reds game to start and I'm having one of my little problems. It's Sammy Davis Junior singing the National Anthem at Riverfront Stadium in Cincinnati and the sound of Sammy's voice bellowing out those words has me all stirred up.

Sammy's building to the climax and I'm wiping away tears. I feel Jocko nudge my knee. I kiss his old forehead then spring up and turn off the TV. I need a shower.

The phone rings while I'm rinsing but I dally and by the time I step out of the tub it stops. Might be Joy calling a day early. Might be Sarah calling to see if we need dog food or something. But I doubt it. The phone woke us this morning and just as Sarah got her leg out of the covers, on the third ring, it quit. Who lets a phone ring only three times?

The Reds are stomping the Astros so I snap off the TV again and retake my position on the couch. I down a mouthful of beer to coat the insides and then light up a number, lean back.

So now I feel better. And here's Sarah bringing in the groceries.

And Jocko barking for his new rawhide bone. I mention the phone call. We speculate about who is calling but it's a puzzle we can't figure out. Then she says, "Let's get out of the house for a while."

"You were just out."

"I mean farther out."

"The mountains?"

"I was thinking the reservation."

That's the Navajo reservation north of the mountains. She likes to shop at the lonesome stands the women set up along the highways. She's crazy about Indian clothing.

"We'll take a cooler of beer and have a sunset picnic."

"You better drive," I say, and she grins indulgently.

Let me mention this. It's background for what I know is coming. A rough period. I hate to but it's important.

I was the first in my family to graduate from college. Did it with the GI Bill. All of my relatives showed up in Austin on commencement day, wearing string ties and Stetsons, sappy summer hats and lots of lace. I was a hero for once in my life. But they wanted more. So I went on to law school. Got a good job.

Two years later when I was fired from the law firm in Houston, one of the partners, Mr. Jacobs, said, "You haven't the instinct for it, William. I've seen it before. Bright young men who just can't cut it when it comes to the doing." He declared me moody and inconsistent, judged against me as a "go-getter," ruled that I was lacking in matters practical.

Humiliation settled into me like a cold settles into the lungs. I wanted never again to see the inside of a law office, never again to speak the language of jurisprudence. For a solid year I would hardly leave the house. In the second year Marge divorced me and returned to Austin with Joy. In the third my dad died of lung cancer; my mom died of grief, and leukemia.

I emerged. I moved. First to Fort Worth where a college friend had a computer business. I kept looking. El Paso. Albuquerque. Santa Fe. In Tucson I got a job taking inventory at Safeway stores in the middle of the night. Work that suited me.

One August day the company sent a team of us up to Flagstaff to inventory a new store, and I decided to stay. It's a pretty town—mountains, the desert. And I met Sarah. She's a psychologist, not my psychologist, but she does some work at the charity hospital here. That's where the police took me the night they found me running naked down a busy thoroughfare. The officials called it an "incident"; my doctor called it manic-depression "finally making itself known in a big way." After six weeks they sent me home with a jar of lithium. Which helps balance my chemicals but I hate the stuff. It's like having to buy air to breathe. It's wrong, like a violation of my rights. As an American, I mean, I ought to be independent . . . don't you think?

So we're on the road. Sarah says, "Oh look," and she steers the car off the highway toward a huge sign: JEWELRY.

The small dark woman behind the crude stand hardly acknowledges our presence as we scan her wares. I watch her watching us from the crate she's sitting on. Whether we buy or not, whether we're dead or alive, she doesn't care. She reminds me of one of Sarah's paintings at home. All about her is an air of ancient deprivation and solitude, oriental resignation, like some of the women I saw in the war. Flies are buzzing around and there's a grubby kid sitting in the dust at the woman's feet next to a box of Church's Fried Chicken bones, the bones bleached white.

Sarah picks out a necklace of blue coral and liquid silver. The women bargain. They reach a price, $15, and I say to Sarah, "Let me get it." I press a $20 bill into the woman's hand before Sarah can protest. "Keep the change," I say and still the woman does not smile. She takes the money, sits on her crate.

In the car Sarah gives me a kiss and thanks me.

"Consider it an engagement present," I say.

She grins, glances over, says nothing.

"You want a beer?" I say, opening one for myself.

It's evening now. We're alone at a little park. Across the desert valley shimmers the sun on a hill like the flame on a match. The scene is vast and awesome. This is what we're here to see, the setting sun, and I understand again why the paintings of Native Americans are so mysterious, so strange.

"Did you take your pill?" Sarah asks and I lie, nod my head.

Sarah puts her elbows on the concrete table and leans against my shoulder. In the ice chest on the ground are the remains of dinner and several beer cans. I light a joint, pass it to her but she shakes her head no, says, "Go easy on that." So I sit and smoke, gaze at the sun, listen to the wind, the silence. The day is winding down. "It's beautiful, so peaceful," she says.

I feel my little problem creeping into my eyes. I don't know for sure but I believe it has something to do with the concept of peace, how I long for it, what it would mean if I found it. The notion sort of overwhelms me with tenderness for myself and for Sarah and for everyone who has ever meant anything to me. Suddenly I miss everyone I have ever known; a parade of faces passes before me. In the sliver of sun that remains I can see my father and mother, my sister, Joy, and even Marge, and even some faces from the war, shimmering images, distant but clear, surrounded by mist and moving away toward a vanishing point like the faces in Indian paintings rising peacefully into the heavens.

"You okay?" Sarah says and I stand up.

"The sun's down," I announce in a croak. "Let's dance."

She looks at me like I'm mad but goes along. I take her hand and help her onto the picnic table and then ease myself up beside her. We smile in the dusk light, move together. I take her in my arms and whisper, "It's that necklace." She pats my shoulder.

2.

We've arrived at Sunday afternoon. Day Two, so to speak. All day I've been anxious, suffering premonitions of ill, certain that something terrible is about to happen. I've worried about Joy, Sarah, even Jocko, won't let either one out of my sight.

"Why doesn't she call?" I ask Sarah.

"Call her," she says, "if you're really worried."

"No. I never call."

She raises an eyebrow accusingly. And it's then that the phone rings. Sarah smiles. I light up and head for the second bedroom, our little office, to talk to my daughter. It rings for the third time as I cross the threshold, and when I snatch up the receiver silence greets me. The line is empty. I slam it down and sit at Sarah's desk, gaze out the window, wondering. There's the flag waving in the breeze at half staff, no knob on the pole, no one paying any attention to it, so I salute, hold it for a moment, and just as I'm snapping my elbow the phone rings again.

"Hey, Mister Daddy," says Joy. "How's it hanging?"

"You shouldn't talk like that to your father."

"Like what?" she says in a tease. She giggles. I snub out my cigarette. Then we talk about the usual stuff. Her mother is fine, her stepfather is out of town on business as usual, the Mercedes is in the shop as usual, school went well this year (As and Bs) and now she is taking swimming lessons and dance lessons and piano lessons. Yes she received my birthday present; no it didn't fit but it will in a couple of years. Her little voice is clear and inviting, like bubbling water.

"Listen," she says. "Mom wanted me to tell you that a man called here looking for you."

"What man?"

"It wasn't for money or anything. He said he knew you from the war. His name was Fred, let me spell it, M-A-R-G-O-L-I-S, from Toledo. We gave him your number."

"Hang on," I say. I go for a smoke and linger coming back.

Let's break in here. Fred Margolis is important to the story. Fred Margolis is the type of man who would let a phone ring only three times. He was in my outfit all the way through. He'd enlisted and would volunteer for anything. Last time I talked to him he was running three successful businesses at the same time. Real estate, appliances, and chickens or something. He owned two houses, several cars. Father to half a dozen kids.

But here's the scoop on Fred Margolis and me: Fred and I killed a man once, face-to-face, on a patrol, at dusk, near a village that our guys later burned to the ground. We'd been close, Fred and I, the closest of buddies but after that I grew to hate him. He talked about it all the time, how the man's grimy face was so dumb with fear and surprise when he met us on the trail and how we beat him to the draw and how Fred got $5 for the watch he lifted from the dead man's wrist. It's funny: I remember the man's surprise, but I recall it as a happy surprise, almost a smile, like for some reason he was glad to see us, like we were all friends; as if he understood something we didn't know about.

It was war, I know. But my idea of the war had been: you go, you keep your head down, do what you're told, you live, you come home. Fred's idea was something else, something I hadn't seen in him stateside. And here's the worst part. Fred tracks me down wherever I go. Every two or three years he calls, at all hours. He yells into the phone: Hey, is this Billy Boy Bosworth of Company B? Then he laughs. Every time it's a letdown, a chore to talk to him. He always asks what I'm "up to," where I've been, and where I'm going. The first time I was in college. The second, law school. The last time, Tucson, he was organizing a reunion of guys in our company, and he reported to me in crazy detail the fates of at least a dozen men, three of whom had since died.

I pick up the phone again and say, "How did he find you?"

"Who? Oh. Beats me," she says. "Maybe he's a spy."

"Did he say anything else?" She indicates no and we go silent for a while. Then Joy says, "Listen, Daddy, when are you coming to Texas? It's been two years, you know. That Christmas."

"I know, darling. I don't know. Maybe this year."

"Well don't wait too long or you won't even recognize me."

"Soon," I lie. "I promise it'll be soon."

Her response is one word, something harsh, and we go silent again, knowing we've said all there is to say. Already I miss her. We hang up. I sit in the chair at the desk. Outside the breeze has slackened and my old flag hangs limp.

The evening news is bad. Connie Chung's pretty face is solemn behind the screen. Sarah and I pick at our food and stare at the TV. The pictures show flag-draped coffins and wailing relatives. More young sailors have died from their wounds; more citizens of Saragosa have been found in the rubble.

My chest is a whirlpool of emotion. It's simple: at this moment I love these people, all of them—the sailors, the crushed children, even Connie Chung and the men reporting the stories from the scenes of devastation. The power of television allows me to share their grief, to hate the message but love the messenger. I have read that in some cultures such emotion can build to the point that brothers leap into graves begging to be buried alive with their loved ones and that mothers actually pluck out their eyes to prevent them having to see the empty world any longer.

Ours is not such a culture; we prefer memorials, quiet and somber. To grieve alone, inside, with dignity. Tomorrow, I know, on Memorial Day, there will be pictures of quiet solitary Americans standing before the black granite wall of the Vietnam War Memorial in Washington. We'll see men in faded field jackets touching the chiseled names of their dead buddies; we'll see praying sisters dressed in black, children who never knew their fathers, wives without husbands, fathers without sons. I couldn't do it; I could never go to Washington and touch the stone.

Then something comes to me, a great idea, a humanitarian effort. "I've just decided," I say to Sarah. "I'm going to Saragosa. I'm going to help with the disaster relief."

"I'm sure they have plenty of help," she says. "Besides you have to work on Tuesday. And how would you get there?" She has a point. Just now I'm without a car; we always use hers. She touches my hand across the table. She says, "You okay?" And here it comes: the little problem.

"Did you take your pill today?"

I lie: nod yes. It's been days now, weeks.

"Don't look at me, please," I say, standing up.

The cold water feels good, the familiar smell of the bathroom reassures me, but my face in the mirror repulses me. The red watery eyes, the ugly wrinkles, the quivering chin. This is no way for a man to act. Certainly not in the presence of a woman who already has her doubts. I want to break something, anything. I look around for something to break, see nothing worth it and return to my face in the mirror. Which is even uglier now, now that I want to break something.

Sarah is leaning over me, her face wrenched with concern. I'm on the floor. Shards of glass are everywhere. The memory of a sound like crashing dishes thrums in my ears and a pain pulses through my hand, up my arm. "You're bleeding," she says, but her voice seems far away and receding. She wraps my hand in a towel, says something about the hospital, says to lie still.

"No hospital," I say.

Sarah is a blurry image hovering above me. Then her image blurs completely and I'm someplace far away in my mind, a place I've been before. I can see it as clearly as ever, clearly as if I were back in the war and it was fifteen years ago and that dead Charlie in his black pajamas was lying on the ground at my feet again with that look still on his grimy face like he understands something I don't know about. It's a look of great relief, as if he's just broken wind or received his discharge papers. Even though he's dead! I mean, the man is dead but I have questions. *There's something I've been wanting to know for a long time . . . what are you smiling about?* This time he lifts his head so he can see me. His expression goes serious. And then, in perfect English, he says, *I'm not smiling.* Simple as that.

So I push on. I say, *Well why were you so happy when we met on the trail? When we killed you, I mean. Can you tell me?* He raises his head again. He says, *Happy?* The thought of it makes him almost smile again as if he is happily surprised that I asked. He says only, *You'll see.* Then he lays his head down, lets out a sigh and slips into a peaceful sleep. I push on. *What did you mean by that, that I'll see? When will I see?* He says nothing. His face is blank now. "Tell me," I yell and I reach out to shake him. Instead of that man though it's Sarah I'm shaking.

The phone is ringing again, wavering up the hall and right into bed with us. "Don't answer it," I say. Four rings, maybe five, then the house is quiet, empty, calm once more. We lie together in silence for a long time until I'm lucid again. I recall the scene in the bathroom, Sarah helping me to bed. "In the morning we better find a doctor for that hand."

"It's only a cut," I say.

"At the hospital," she says. "Just to be safe."

"Sure," I say but then it comes to me what she's up to. It makes me smile, what she's up to. While my hand is being doctored she'll sneak away and find the resident psychiatrist. She'll explain my recent behavior and ask him to talk to me. He'll come into the room, very cheerful, ask questions (how am I feeling? am I taking my medication? anything I want to talk about?) and I'll say no because to talk in that way would just bring on the little problem, and I'm sick of the little problem. I want it to go away along with this rough period and I don't want to need the pills anymore. I can live without them. A success.

The thought of success gets my mind to going full-speed. I start to see things. A life for myself. It would be a simple life. What I want is simple. I want peace and to work steadily, and I want a yard of my own to tend, and I want to know that every morning when I get up Sarah will be there with a greeting and all we'll ever talk about is the future, of the planting of shrubs and flowers, of the dogs we want to raise, of payroll deductions and savings accounts and retirement plans. There's a job at a landscaping nursery I've been thinking about; it would be good work, outside in the good fresh air.

Sarah is talking about how I need to watch my drinking and my smoking, start getting some exercise, but I interrupt her. "Marry me, Sarah," I say toward the ceiling.

She lets a sigh escape into the room. She shifts her body under the covers. She says, again, "We'll see," and I know what it means. We lie still, breathing quietly now. I reach out and she takes my hand and I feel myself drifting, slipping away, not into sleep but into something that is not like sleep at all.

3.

We have a big hole at this point. In the story, I mean. I'll have to reconstruct it. So call this a reconstruction project.

First let me set the scene. Everything is mustard yellow. The room is perhaps 20x20. There's a window with mini-blinds. There's a door, wide, institutional, with no handle. Outside the door is a gathering of people dressed in robes, old clothes, a night-gown. They shuffle by, heads bent, smoking, pondering. Wily laughter can be heard and the acrimonious voices of two men arguing. They're all fruitcakes on the ward.

It's Tuesday evening. Apparently I missed Memorial Day altogether. I'm in the hospital, and I'm trying to understand what has happened to me. Apparently, Sarah says, I waited until she was asleep again, and then sometime after midnight I drew myself up and got out of bed. I propped open the front door and quietly took all the dining room chairs outside, put them in a circle on the lawn. "Like for a conference, or something," she said, adding that on the ground in the center of the circle I carefully stacked a dozen large stones from the driveway. "Like a monument, or something." Next, apparently, I started walking. Old Jocko followed. Four miles I walked, barefoot, unmolested and molesting no one, along streets with broken glass, through fields with ragged brambles, under street lights and over bridges until I walked right into an all-night Big Boy restaurant on the interstate. Jocko, apparently, stayed with me all the way.

"You were wrapped in your flag," Sarah said. "As if it were a cape or an Indian blanket. And you were carrying the pole like a walking stick. At first they thought you'd been to a costume party. But it didn't take them long to see. You were shivering. Your feet were bleeding. And you refused to let them take the dog outside. He snapped at someone who tried to touch you. You kept mumbling, 'You'll see, you'll see,' and saluting everyone."

Apparently the people in the restaurant were kind to me. They put a coat over my shoulders and gave me lemon pie to eat and some coffee to drink and they called the police, who also were kind to me. This time at least, she said, I was wearing underwear. "Were they clean?" I asked. Sarah smiled, patted my arm on the hospital cot. "See," she said. "You'll be fine."

She told me this during visiting hours. Her hair was done, she was wearing a business suit: she'd come by after work. The doctors, she said, want me for one more day before they'll release me to Sarah's care . . . if I'll take my medicine.

Through the window I can see the lights of Flagstaff. The lights are all moving in rhythm, sliding around and leaving behind little tails of light. The shakes is the worst part. For weeks I'll be thirsty and walk like a cripple and sleep a lot.

Here's Sarah coming into the room. She has a tote bag and a cheerful face for the sick one, a handful of wildflowers.

"You bring me some smokes?" I ask.

"Yes," she says indulgently. "I brought cigarettes."

"You bring me some lovin'?" I ask and she just smiles.

⁂

On Thursday I'm up and waiting for Sarah by seven o'clock. There's a creepy domesticity about the room: my personal belongings all about—shaving kit, picture of Jocko, box of Kleenex—Sarah's flowers on the table and a bunch from my boss Johnny. I shuffle around in my paper slippers, finishing up, checking myself in the window's reflection. I'm excited. It's a thrill, going on a journey, leaving someplace, starting out early.

Sarah shows about eight along with an orderly and a wheelchair. Fruitcakes clap and cheer as the orderly rolls me out. The day is fresh and clean. On the road I watch the traffic: pickups speeding by and cars carrying white-shirted men to their offices. I should be at work. Sarah says, "I talked to Johnny and he said for you to just come on in again whenever you're feeling better."

At home Sarah leads me by the hand as we put away my things, settle me in again. She talks about taking everything one step at a time. She has prepared a bed on the couch so I can watch TV while I rest. I sit on the couch, my hands tremble, I smoke.

"Well," she says. "I need to get on to work. You okay?"

"Finer than frog hair," I say, gazing up at her, and it's then I notice she's wearing her new necklace, our necklace.

When she leaves I get up and shuffle through the house. With Jocko at my heels I straighten pictures, fluff the bed, and there on the dresser is the flag waiting for me, folded, silent. From its closet I take the ladder and set it up under the hole in the ceiling. I'm hoping for a minor triumph, to negotiate the ladder by myself and put away the flag and renegotiate the ladder to safety. The ascent is no problem though I'm a little woozy once I push open the plywood cover and stand up. I poke through the MISC box, handle the diplomas, replace the flag.

Suddenly I'm very tired. I lie down on the floorboards and stretch out, my slippers dangling above the hole in the ceiling.

Soon I start to doze, and at first I'm not sure I hear the phone ringing down below. I don't move, don't even open my eyes. Three rings is all I get. Maybe next time I'll answer. It comes to me then; I can see it. I'd hurry into the office, sit at the desk, light a smoke, pick up the receiver, hold it to my ear.

I'd say, Hello, Fred. And he'd say, Is this Billy Boy Bosworth of Company B? Then he'd laugh. And I'd say, Sure, Fred, it's me. And he'd say, Gosh, buddy, where the hell've you been?

When It's a House

My daddy—at forty I still call him Daddy, we all do, even my brother, the executive, who is forty-six—Daddy is once again marking off the spot I've chosen for my house. My "cabin," he calls it.

I sit on the tailgate of my pickup in the shade of a live oak tree and watch him as he paces the back wall, one foot at a time, one boot placed carefully in front of the other. At thirty feet he stops, looks up thinking about something, mutters a mental note to himself, then he turns and moves along the side wall where my little kitchen and the bathroom will be. When he gets to twenty-four he stops again, thinks again, and then starts along the front wall where I'm planning a picture window and a big porch to catch the view. Through it all he's calculating.

Something about this is so familiar to me that it's like watching a home movie from my childhood. It's like we're at home, the whole family, over in Houston, some special occasion, and when the one with the camera says, "Okay, do something entertaining," Daddy, out of the habits of his working life, gets a distracted look in his eyes and then paces off the dimensions of a building, any building, right there on the front yard. It's about the only kind of entertainment he has ever known. He was a builder of houses, and he did all right by himself. Now he is retired.

He is sixty-nine years old. He is bright, he is strong. He is willful and vain. He is frightened of dying. Since he quit smoking, after four stays at the hospital in two years, he has put on weight, forty pounds worth, and you'd think he'd been caught mooning the governor. He says, patting his belly, "Isn't this awful." He says, "You seen the basketball lately?" He is hard on himself. He says, "The baby's due any day now, and I like cigars." I just smile over it and mention how healthy he looks.

It's true. There's a lot of new life in his eyes, his ruddy skin, his smile with the stained teeth. He still has all his hair but it's a mass of white now, like his beard. When he retired, early, he went western on us. Bought some land up north of Houston, bought some cows, bought a few horses, bought an old guy's Stetson and some Tony Lamas. For a few years it was grand. We'd all show up at Christmas or the Fourth of July—my brother with his clan, my sister with hers—and we'd ride, we'd poke the cows, we'd talk about developing the land, more clearing and fencing, that sort of thing. We had picnics and played horseshoes.

Then he got sick and the scare set in, and he decided to consolidate his holdings. He sold everything but the house and one old horse, the family favorite, who now lives on a friend's ranch. About then came the awful change: something clicked or fizzled; something frazzled or dazzled. Now it's like having a Gabby Hayes with brains hanging around, an amusing character, a bumpkin sidekick. His hair is bushy and his beard is scraggly and for about a year he's been wearing a UT gimme cap with scrambled eggs on the bill like a trailer-park general's. He wears denim overalls that haven't faded out right yet. He wears wire-rimmed bifocals, crooked on his nose.

He chews Skoal and sucks on lollipops. He says "ya-hoo" too often and things like "hell to breakfast" and "month of Sundays," and he laughs with an oddwad yucking tic in his voice at inconvenient times. A sad transformation.

Daddy has finished pacing off the house. He scratches something on his notepad and then sits beside me on the tailgate. For a good long moment there's nothing but silence, a kind of peace, a calm as generous as the country we're looking at, all cedar and scrub oak and startling limestone jags against the distant ridges. Close your eyes and open them quick: it's like mountains. Like being right up in the gentle peaks with nothing around you but the wind. And the sky . . . so huge, so blue.

My daddy looks at his notepad. He looks at me. He says, "Don't you think this cabin ought to be a little bigger?"

"No sir I don't." I light up a cigarette.

He frowns. "And you're sure this is where you want it?"

"Positive."

"It's more level down there," he says, pointing.

"But the view's up here I keep telling you."

He grunts a deep one and then smiles with indulgence. He tugs on my ponytail. He sniffs the cloud of smoke I make. He says, "Okay, Padna, you're the boss." Then, for no apparent reason, he lets out with one of his new tics: "Yip yip yip aw-haaa," sort of a variation on a Bob Wills' yodel. His face shows a curious kind of delight. We sit on the tailgate, swinging our boots, gazing over the hills at the ten-mile view, broad and rambling and without conflict in the early morning haze.

But I hear what he's thinking: *Why me? Why, of all the sons on earth, did I get this one?* I have no ambition, he thinks, and he is not far from right. If he's in a charitable mood his line goes: *He's a smart kid but he doesn't use good sense . . . must have been the war and all those drugs*. An old excuse.

I'm a veteran from way back, one of the last draftees. After that I traveled and moved around the country for years before settling in Texas again. With my benefits I went to college and then to work as the manager of a bookstore in Austin, but when the city hit half a million I got free of it. With my benefits I bought this piece of land, twelve acres, way out in the Hill Country. I have taken a job at the feed store in a small town nearby. I work four tens. Fridays I read in my garage apartment at the widow Graber's. Saturdays I clear cedar here on the land and then make the long drive into Austin. Saturday nights and Sundays are for my girlfriend, Alicia. With my father's help I am going to build a house, and my hope is that Alicia will then leave Austin and live here with me. My plan is to fence the land, make pastures, build pens and a barn, raise animals. My family doesn't understand this. They wonder why I live so far away; they wonder why I'm wasting my education; they wonder why I'm not married.

I can never answer.

Daddy wonders too but he is "honored" that I asked him to help, "tickled" to have something to do, "proud" to be a builder of houses once more, and he's afraid I'll send him away if he starts in on me. For the next two months, as we have planned it, he'll drive over from Houston on Thursday, room with me at the widow Graber's, work hard for three days, then drive home again on Monday. To him, I think, it's like a great adventure.

"Listen," I say. "Are you sure you're up to all this?"

"You bet ya, Boss. When do we start?"

"How's about right now?"

His eyes flare. "Yip yip yip aw-haaa," he yodels and then he starts groping in the bed of the truck for his hammer.

First we build a form for the foundation. This takes two weekends, six days. We dig up the earth with the rented backhoe, we make batter boards, we lay water lines, septic lines, we wait for a load of river sand; we lay rebar and iron mesh for support, and my site is on a dangerous incline.

"Boy I'll tell ya," he says about a dozen times. "Down there we'd have this finished and the concrete poured already."

"But this is where I want it. Will you quit with that?"

His look is fat with wisdom and doubt but all he says is, "Okay, Padna," in a small exhausted voice.

By Monday morning when he is ready to leave for Houston we are both tired out and bone sore and have little to say over breakfast at the Tally-Ho Cafe. During the week I rest and read a lot, talk to Alicia on the phone at night. When he returns on Thursday, in time for supper at Big John's, which he pays for, our spirits have lifted again. He's done some new calculating. We're ready for the concrete which comes early Friday morning.

"That's quite a climb," says the truck driver when he gets out. His name is Manuel. We exchange howdies and what have you and then Manuel says, "Wouldn't it be more level down there?"

"Well, yeah, it would," Daddy says. "But we want it here."

Manuel shrugs. He is middle-aged, short and stout and neatly dressed in his workingman's blue uniform. His job is to deliver and pour concrete, but getting the foundation level is important to a house, and it's very hard work for just two men. And when the touchy part comes, Manuel takes Daddy's place, helping with the shovel, the striking board, the bull float, working up a bad sweat. Daddy gives him a twenty-dollar tip for his trouble.

"You're going to build this house all by yourselves?" Manuel is hot and skeptical. He sizes up Daddy and then, looking at me, his eyes ask: *With just this old guy?*

"That's right," Daddy answers, panting hard and stooped with pain. "And it'll be the best house in the county too."

Manuel offers good luck, more like condolences, and tries to give back the twenty dollars. Daddy won't take it. There's a brief but friendly dispute, very embarrassing, before Manuel gets in the truck and rumbles away. It's then, in that powerful silence, that Daddy lies down in the cab of his pickup and puts a wet towel over his eyes, even though I know from my reading there's still much to do before the concrete starts to dry.

"You okay?" I ask.

"Yeah fine. Be with you in a minute."

It's an hour-and-a-half before he emerges. By then I have done all I can by myself with the finishing trowel, the edger, the wood float to make my new floor smooth and even and level. My knees ache and my palms are pocked by bits of gravel.

"Gosh, Buddy, sorry I pooped out on you."

His eyes are red and glassy, his face pale; he looks hangdog and pitiful in his muddy overalls. He takes a long drink from the Igloo cooler, swallows a pill of some sort, sits on a saw horse.

"How's it look?" I ask.

"Super, super. Yeah. It looks great, you did good."

But I know better. There are swirls and hollows and an unplumbness to it all. The level square is a cruel but truthful master and its bubble tells me the floor of my house will forever tilt toward Abilene. We gaze at the slab of concrete, my new foundation, and I see again this is not going to be easy.

"Look here, Hoss, I'm sorry—"

"Don't worry about it, Daddy. Let's get some lunch."

In the afternoon we go to the lumberyard in town to buy the first load of framing materials. The lumberyard is one of these new places, a cavernous metal warehouse with most of the wood neatly displayed in racks at the back of the store. We take a long time with our selecting, checking every two-by-four against warp and curl. "Yeah yeah yeah," he chortles with a Rube's excitement each time we settle on a good one. We trundle everything to the front on two loud, rambling carts. At the checkout counter, when the nice woman has tallied it all, Daddy insists on paying. We argue quietly. I tell him I've been saving for this for years. I tell him I have all the money I'll need set aside in a special account at the local bank. This is my house we're building.

"Your mother and I would like to do this for you," he says in a whisper. "At least some of it. You should have a place."

"But I'm doing this for myself."

"I'm not saying you can't," he whispers loudly. "All's I'm saying is we'd like to help."

The woman at the counter, a puffed blonde about my age with an unfortunate cleft in her nose, has to wait while we argue. She tries not to watch, not to listen, but her shy smile implies that she knows and understands the ways of parents. He's got his checkbook out; it's on the counter; now he's ignoring me.

"Will you take a check on a Houston bank?"

"All the same to me," she says, smiling at him like he's an eccentric old gentleman, which he is. "Long as it's good."

"Oh it's good, young lady. How much is it?"

"Six-hundred eight-two dollars and ninety-seven cents."

He hesitates; the woman and I see the astonishment in his eyes, in his hand with the pen poised above the checkbook. He laughs, that odd, low yucking sound. It stops abruptly. He eyes her through the top of his bifocals. "How much?"

She tells him again, deadpan and business-like. He whistles through his teeth, says something like, "Whoa now, hawse," so I step in. I say, "I told you, Daddy, I'll pay for it."

"No no, that's fine. Super. We want to do this for you."

He writes out a check. As always this is a very slow process with him. He writes in block letters, squarish little numerals, calculating each one, and his signature is a wild flourish that no one can read. The woman and I exchange a glance, share the shame of children, and before he gets the receipt from her I am pushing one of the carts out the door to the parking lot.

My beautiful hill now looks like a real construction site. All around are stacks of lumber, a table saw under a jerry-rigged shelter, the left-over sand in a dented pile. The slab is a dull fish color in the afternoon sunshine. There is nothing to do now but wait. The slab has to cure, to dry. We decide he might as well go on home; we'll start framing next week. "Keep that lumber dry," he says. On Saturday I drive into Austin.

"How's my poor tired boy?" Alicia wants to know. She is a good woman, a few years younger than I, married once long ago. Her hair is dark, her face a pretty oval, her eyes sharp and light like candle flames. There's enough of her for a man to hold on to, and it's that softness about her that makes it all so comfortable. She'd be my wife if I asked, I think, and we talk about it from time to time, but so far neither of us has asked.

"Papas are always like that," she says when I tell her about Daddy, tell her about my doubts. "Now put out that cigarette."

"Maybe I should just hire a couple of guys to help me."

"Oh no, it wouldn't be the same. No. You let your papa help. He's old and wants to know his boy before he dies. It could come any day, you know, and then you'll have the rest of your life to be a man. Besides he has expertise, experience. Don't you want your house to be nice?"

"But what if I murder him?"

"No. Oh no." She grins. "That's been done before."

Alicia does not like to follow in the paths of others; and she thinks we find truth in the mistakes of our lives. She is a state welfare agent and studies human mistakes. At home, a tiny apartment, she beads earrings, necklaces, hat bands—brightly colored things—and sells them on weekends at crafts shows out in the county. In my house I am planning a small room for her, a workshop. With this I hope to entice her away from the city.

"When can I come see your house?"

"When it's a house," I say.

She smiles and kisses me. She takes my hand. We go out for barbecue at a beer garden near the capitol. We drink beer under the dim lights in the trees and scratch our initials into the wood of the picnic table. We eat red beans and potato salad and greasy pork ribs until our faces are smeared with sauce. We kiss, licking at the sauce, and we place slices of dill pickle on each other's tongue. The band plays C&W with an occasional fifties tune and once our ribs have settled we dance, slow waltzes and two-steps and even a polka. By two a.m. we're the only ones on the floor. It's all easy stuff now, the boys in the band are lazy and quiet and ready for home, and we're doing the one-step. I'm careful of my boots against her sandals. We hold each other close, shuffle about, full of longing and friendship. Her softness is like a promise by the time the band is packing up.

"Well?" I whisper, bending to her ear.

"Well what?" she whispers back, almost asleep.

"You want to get married?"

She lays her head against my chest. She loops her thumbs through my belt loops. She says, "Not really," and then we're like strangers with each other for the rest of the weekend.

The framing goes smoothly, nothing but sawing and lifting and hammering. We wear nail pouches and smell like animals and our hair is always yellow with sawdust. Two weeks—we have the skeletons of walls—and now we are ready for the roof beam.

"All right now, Pancho," says Daddy. "We got to do some serious figuring. Got to get this thing right."

He figures and figures, trying to correct for the sloping foundation. He spits Skoal into a styrofoam cup. He sucks on lollipops. He has overworked; his white hair is wild under his general's cap, and the cuffs of his crazy blue overalls drag the floor. Still he's strong; he's determined. He's up and down off the ladder; he's at the workbench scratching out numbers, writing new ones, adding, subtracting, mumbling to himself. I make a few suggestions but he never listens. My job is to hold the other end of the tape measure or the board or the string and to answer a rare question, such as, "What's fifty-eight and three-fifths minus thirteen and five-eights?" I wait for long stretches.

I sit on my foundation at the place where the front door will be. I look at my view. I smoke cigarettes. It's a Sunday, very quiet out here in the hills. A buzzard wheels about on the currents. The sky is blue, the clouds enormous and gentle. A breeze is blowing and the scent of the cedars is sweet as Christmastime. Very suddenly like a wound I miss Alicia. I want to see her, to smell her, to talk to her. Nothing much, just a "Hi, how are ya?" I get an image of her in my mind as clear as any home movie. She's right out there, stepping from her car. She waves and then she is walking up the hill under the oaks. She's wearing a light frail dress and sandals on her feet and a silver bracelet on her arm and her hair is free in the wind and her legs are like a pretty song and her neck is like a poem. And then she is sitting here with me, happy and calm, glancing around like a little bird asking about the wall plate and the door hanger and asking me with a lovely smile, "Is it a house yet?"

"Not quite," I say.

"Oh! Is that my room?"

I nod my head.

"So when can we move in?" she wants to know, but I can't answer. Then it's just me and my view again.

"Yip yip yip aw-haaa," Daddy yodels.

This means he is ready, he has figured it out. I drag myself up and we go back to work. We struggle, him on one ladder, me on the other, trying to get the roof beam plumb and secured to a couple of support posts. We measure, make our marks, tack it up, check the level square, tap it loose, try again.

"You gotta hold it steady, son," he says, his glasses crooked, sweat streaming down his face.

We try it again. Still it's off.

"You got to hold it steady, son. How many times I gotta tell ya? Let's start over."

We tap it loose. We measure again. We make our marks. Up the ladders we go, hoisting the heavy roof beam. We lift it above our heads; our arms tremble. Carefully, steadily I hold it while he tacks up his end. Steadily I hold it while I tack up mine.

"How's it look?" he says.

"Looks good to me."

Down he goes. He moves the ladder to the center of the house. At his feet are scraps of lumber, hand saws lying about, bent nails, footprints in the sawdust. Up he goes, carrying the level square. He clamps it to the wood, he ogles the bubble and I can tell by his disgusted eyes that it's off again.

"Shoot fire!" he hollers. "How many times I gotta tell you: *hold it steady*. We're gonna get this right even if it kills me."

By now I'm mad, I'm sick of it all, and I say something to him that I've never said before: "I've had enough of this shit."

"What's that?"

"I ain't no boy, Daddy, and you ain't no job foreman and if I'd gotten some help with the foundation we wouldn't be having this problem."

His old face shows injury; the slump of his body shows fatigue and defeat. He searches the floor as if looking for a weapon. Then he looks up at me on my ladder.

"Well fine," he says. "If that's the way you feel about it then I'll just go on home right now."

"Maybe that'd be the best."

"Maybe it would."

"Fine."

"Fine."

"You won't see me again you know."

"Fine."

We offer each other cold-blooded glares before turning away and it's then he says, "You gotta grow up, son."

I just snort a laugh and keep still.

He looks around, finds his circle saw, unplugs it from the extension cord and holds it close under his arm. He finds his hammer. He moves heavily over the tools and the lumber lying on the floor. He eases himself off the slab. He walks to his pickup and drops his tools inside. He unties his nail pouch and throws it toward the table saw. He gets in his truck and starts it. The truck idles for a long time before he puts it in gear. Then he is gone. Through all of this I've been sitting on the top of my ladder, just watching, listening. When the growl of his truck has faded out among the hills I curse a good riddance, a nice loud one, and without thinking I strike out at something with heel of my hand. The roof beam goes crashing to the floor.

So I'll go on alone, I think on Monday, hire some guys to help me. I eat at the Tally-Ho, work seven to six, read in my room. I sleep a lot. Tuesday I change my mind; I don't want a house, none of it, all that responsibility, the expense. Maybe I'll travel again. This comes to me on Wednesday and I imagine a trip out West, nights in the tent, days on the road, plenty of time to wander. I plug in my phone and call Alicia but when her answering machine clicks on I hang up. That night in the glow of a lantern I hammer a For Sale sign to a tree in front of my house.

On Thursday, without calling, without letting me know, Daddy shows up again just like nothing has happened. He's sitting high up on the stoop of my apartment sucking a toothpick when I come home from supper. Leaning against the door is my For Sale sign.

"I stopped by out at the site," he says. "We can lick this thing. No mistakes this time. I figured a new way to do it."

I stand on the steps below him and listen. Something about him has changed, something fundamental but obvious, and it takes me a moment to see what it is. He's gotten a haircut; his beard is trim, his neck clean. He's wearing khaki trousers with a new leather belt around his bulgy waist and on the stoop behind him lies his old guy's good Stetson. He even smells of aftershave, something sweet and cheap from his grandchildren. For the first time in years he looks more or less like himself, but older and worn out and somehow vulnerable. Of course it's my fault.

"Listen, Daddy, I'm sorry—"

"Don't worry about it, Hoss."

We look at each other for a long time, and understand. We'll go on with the house, we'll see, we'll finish it.

"Oh! Some cookies your sister made," he says and holds out a tinfoil bundle. I sit on the stoop beside him. He takes a pack of Viceroys from his pocket and offers it to me along with some matches. I slip one out, light it, hand the package back to him but he shakes his head no and tells me to keep it.

"I only smoked one," he says. "Don't tell your mother."

We glance sideways, we grin, we glance away. We talk in that familiar after-dinner way of fathers and sons. We have nowhere to go, nothing to do but talk. I smoke and he sniffs the cloud I make and after a while I offer again, shaking the pack at him. This time, with a shrug, he accepts.

"Just one more," he says.

He savors the taste, the feel of it, rolling it between his fingers as he would a fine cigar and he coughs a quick little blast each time he exhales. I keep offering and he keeps taking. He shouldn't, but this is the way of men and we both know it.

So we sit there and smoke as the dusk comes on and then deepens, becomes tender, talking about nothing in particular, talking about roof beams and wood siding and wallboard, talking about dimensions and strategy, talking in low voices and muttered grunts, until the phone rings inside. It's like a jarring pulse in the atmosphere. We turn our heads to listen. I know who it is; four weeks it's been and I'm sure she's wondering. *Where have you been?* she'll want to know. *Are you okay? And your papa? Have you murdered him? Is it a house yet?* All those questions.

"A man should answer his phone," my daddy says but I keep still, keep silent, biding my time. Then the ringing stops.

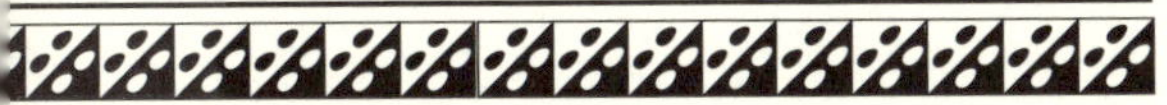

Naming Mansfield

Edward Mansfield, the prize-winning journalist, has had a hard day and would like to soak in his hot tub. But the hot tub is out of commission, has been since Christmas. He believes the fault lies in the electricity, the very idea of which frightens him. Everybody knows that water and electricity don't go together without danger and he has been hesitant to test his luck lately.

He bought the hot tub at a garage sale the summer he and Marcia were restoring the old house. Those were the good days, back before Marcia quit her job to take up painting and sculpturing full time. An artist is supposed to be crazy, he figures, and he had expected controlled lunacy, strange talk and late nights and weird people dropping by; he had not expected her to tell him she didn't love him anymore and take off for days at a time. She says she's out looking for inspiration and material, but he knows better: must be another man.

There's a piece of her work on the patio. It's an old floor lamp, denuded of all its lamp parts, with lengths of angle iron welded at right angles across the top so that it has "shoulders," as she has explained. Hanging from the angle iron are all kinds of things: antique shoes, a couple of old toasters, a bread box, a roasting pan and other such domestic items. It's all painted bright gold, like the sun. The title of this piece, she says, is FREEDOM or A MODERN-DAY SUNSET. She can't decide which.

Eddie slams one of the toasters to make it all clank together, hoping it will chip the expensive paint. Then he steps off the patio into his summer-deep Bermuda grass and slogs the fifteen feet to the hot tub, just for a look. The redwood deck he built with such care is cracked and disjointed at the corners, a risk to stand on, and the padded top, badly faded and torn now, lies off to the side so that half the tub is open to the sky. There's a beer can floating in the thick covering of scum and something else. He pokes the something else with a finger and then yanks his hand away. It's a dead squirrel, bloated and hard.

"So that's what's been stinking around here," he says.

He goes into the house to wash death off his hands. At the bathroom sink he blinks back tears thinking of that dead squirrel in his hot tub and how it must have struggled toward the end.

Time to call Matt.

Eddie's best friend is trying to be a writer. His name, oddly, is Matt Mansfield. Back when they both worked at the newspaper this created a great deal of confusion. The city editor for instance would yell across the newsroom, "Hey, Mansfield," and they'd both look up, start to rise to see what he wanted. The editor would then get flustered and yell, "No no, not both of you, just the big fart." That meant Eddie. They don't look at all alike—Eddie is large and fair, Matt about average and dark—an ironic fact which still disturbs some people.

"So, are you related?" a woman asked not long ago.

Eddie said, "Yeah he's my son," and then looked at her in such a way that the woman felt stupid for asking.

Since he and Carolyn split up Matt has been living in a cabin in the hills out near Austin. He teaches freshman composition part-time at the community college there and spends the rest of his day staring at his word processor. His hair is long now, he's grown a beard, his eyes are sad and hard-bitten.

Eddie takes his portable phone out to the porch and punches in Matt's number. Matt always answers: "Earth here."

"It's me," Eddie says. "She's gone again."

Matt takes this in and says, "Where'd she go?"

"Out West, I think."

Eddie hears a lighter click, an exhalation of breath.

"Did I interrupt something? You working?"

"Naw, not really. I'm gonna get started again on Monday."

"Good. You know I support you in what you're doing."

Matt says, "Did Marcia say when she was coming home?"

"Nope. And on top of everything Mateo is missing again."

Mateo is Eddie's dog, a foundling that Marcia named after Matt because it was Matt who found him. He was still in Houston then; he came over for breakfast one day and the dog followed him right inside. Mateo is a fine companion. He has a brindle coat and ears of a magnificent sort that stand out at right angles to his head as if he's always listening for trouble. He is affectionate and bright and strong, an acrobat who can stand flat-footed and leap a four-foot fence. Which is why he's missing.

"Have you looked for him?" Matt asks.

"Not yet. He'll come home, he always has, but I'm afraid he's gonna get squashed by a truck one of these days."

"Well then why don't we raise your fence? Make it a six- footer. You been talking about it for months."

"Can you come down this weekend?"

"You got two hammers?"

"I got twenty hammers."

"Well there you have it. See you tomorrow afternoon."

"You sure?"

"No. But I'll be there anyway. About suppertime."

Eddie sits there for a while, trying to decide what he'll have for supper, until he hears something strange in his neighbor's yard. It's a scrabbling sound, a clawing at the fence. Soon Mateo's lean head starts to appear, off and on, as if he is jumping on a trampoline. The poor dog is exhausted from his adventures. As Mateo pants hotly and licks his face in thanks, Eddie helps him over the fence and carries him to the house. He gives him a beer in his bowl to cool and calm him down. Then he feeds him and, save a closely guarded excursion down the street to a vacant lot for an after-dinner busy-busy—Marcia's term—he doesn't let him out again all night long.

Friday is a good day, the best day ever invented. It is the day of closure, and of possibilities. Eddie takes off early and goes home. He mows the lawn in a kind of furious, sweaty haste and then drives to Builders Square for the first load of fencing materials. He sees Matt's Ford pickup parked at the curb as soon as he turns the corner onto Mercy Lane North. Both doors are wide open and a booming kind of classical music from the truck's stereo is disturbing the peace of the neighborhood.

When Eddie pulls in the driveway Matt lifts himself and tumbles out of the truck, followed by a crushed beer can that clatters against the curb. They meet on the freshly mown grass of Eddie's front yard, embrace like a couple of grizzly bears.

"How was the drive?"

"I made real good time," Matt says, grinning handsomely in his beard. Matt's not drunk but he's close to it, and Eddie sees he'll have to change his fencing plans. They'll start tomorrow.

In the chilly house Matt greets Mateo in his usual elaborate way. He dances with him, gets him to do some tricks, such as *Be a dead dog*, and then he goes to the kitchen for a dog treat. "I just *love* that dog," Matt says in a high feminine voice, mimicking the estranged Carolyn, and Eddie smiles at his mockery.

On the patio with beers they sit in lawn chairs. Matt looks tired. His hair is a mess and his jeans are torn. Eddie, in his khaki walking shorts and new sneakers, feels neat and clean next to Matt. He thinks he should change; he thinks Matt may consider him too bourgeois to be the best friend of a serious writer.

They talk for a while, catching up, then Matt asks if he's heard from Marcia. Eddie says she called earlier from Santa Fe.

"Wanted to use my Visa card for her hotel bills."

"Y'all argue?"

"Of course we argued."

Eddie starts on his second beer and Matt suggests a soak in the hot tub. Eddie explains why that's impossible.

"Oh," says Matt. "Well what do you feel like doing?"

"Nothing much really, how about you?"

"First a shower, and then a good meal wouldn't hurt me . . . . Listen," says Matt, and Eddie can tell something's coming. "I'm kind of broke. Could you loan me a little for a few days?"

"Of course," Eddie says and Matt thanks him so many times it becomes embarrassing. For a long time they sit and stare into the yard as Eddie tries to calculate his dwindling bank balance.

They shower and dress and then leave for supper in Matt's truck. At an ATM Eddie gives Matt fifty dollars, then they drive on to a steakhouse that Eddie likes. In the parking lot of the restaurant Eddie stops Matt before he gets out.

"Look here," he says. "I want you to do me a favor."

"You name it."

"I want you to start calling me Frank. It's my middle name."

"I know but what's wrong with Eddie all of a sudden?"

"I'm even going to change my by-line to Frank Mansfield."

"Are you gonna tell me why?"

Eddie feels himself blush. He hesitates before committing himself: "Marcia thinks Eddie is stupid."

Matt smirks and glances at Eddie as if he too thinks Eddie is stupid. "What made her decide that after all these years?"

"She says she's never much liked being married to an Eddie. She says it makes me sound like Mr. Ed the horse or that obnoxious guy on Leave it to Beaver. You know, Wally's friend."

"And you listened to her?"

"Yeah. In fact I agree with her. I've always regretted going by Edward instead of Frank." He is afraid to look, afraid of what he'll see, but when he glances over he can't help but return Matt's grin. "I know it's dumb but would you just do it for me?"

"Frank, huh?"

"That's right."

"Frank it is then."

They shake on it and then go inside the restaurant. But Matt won't quit grinning. By the time their meals arrive he can no longer contain himself. He has just put a bite in his mouth when he throws down his silverware with a loud clank and laughs so hard that he spits out a piece of steak. It bounces off the table and lands in Frank's lap. So Frank laughs also now.

"Sorry—Frank," he says. "Would you mind giving me back that piece of steak—Frank. At these prices I don't want to waste it."

Frank picks the slimy chunk of meat out of his napkin and throws it sloppily at Matt's chest. It leaves a gray splatter mark on his white shirt. So they laugh about that too.

Matt says, "I just can't call you Frank, that's all. I've known you too long. Give me time." Suddenly his face brightens with a bright idea. "I know, how about this: let me call you Eddie Frank, as kind of a transition?"

"All right," says Frank. "If you have to. But let me tell you something right now: if you do, if you call me Eddie Frank, like I'm some Billy Jean or James Earl or R.W. or something, then I'm gonna start calling you Matthew Ernest. Agreed?"

Eddie Frank gets up before Matthew Ernest even stirs. He turns off the alarm system they had installed at great expense to protect Marcia's collection of antique baskets, though the two times they've been burglarized the only artifacts the thieves bothered with were televisions and firearms. He feeds Mateo in the kitchen and then supervises his busy-busy in the backyard.

While the coffee is making he goes into the living room and just watches Matthew Ernest sleep for a while. He's sprawled across the couch like a puzzle of himself. He is oblivious and for once peaceful. Thinking about their new and expanded names makes him smile in fondness, makes him want to wake up Matthew Ernest just for the joy of calling him Matthew Ernest and it makes him wish that Marcia were there to be a part of it.

Eddie Frank takes his coffee out to the garage. It's a gray day, threatening rain. Usually on Saturdays he alone or he and Marcia go to garage and estate sales looking for cheap antiques. They have a little business dealing in old things, furniture and books and Western junk. Their shop is a 10x10-foot space in an antiques mall out on the freeway. There is something elegant and fundamental to Eddie Frank in the notion of buying low and selling high, and he's always been something of a scavenger.

Today, however, instead of buying, he's selling. One thing about a small antiques business: you end up owning a lot of stuff that you just can't get rid of. And there's this: since Marcia went crazy she hasn't much felt like being an antiques dealer. In fact one of her complaints is that they have collected "so much shit," as she puts it, they can no longer find the center of their lives for all their material possessions. He can see her point; the garage is so crowded he can't park his Jeep inside.

First he has to make some signs and post them around the neighborhood. He enjoys this part. With a Marks-A-Lot and some squares of yellow posterboard he carefully draws his signs, each one different:

WORLD'S BIGGEST AND BEST GARAGE SALE. HOUSTON'S FINEST GARAGE SALE. STUPENDOUS GARAGE SALE. GOD'S OWN GARAGE SALE. Then he sets out on foot with a staple gun.

Early morning is his thinking time. Lately, it seems, about all he can think about is Marcia. He's thinking about the first time he realized he loved her. This was years ago. He was wild and irresponsible then, living in a seedy little second-floor apartment. He remembers he was in bed, almost asleep, when he heard the voice of someone yelling outside: "Hey, Mansfield."

He went to the door and found Marcia standing at the bottom of the stairs. In her arms was the sleeping bag he had given her for her birthday so they could go camping together.

"Here," she said. "I think this is yours."

She heaved that sleeping bag all the way up to the landing where it lighted heavily at his feet. He was so stunned by this show of strength that he could do nothing but smile at her.

"You are a selfish fucking bastard, you know that," she screamed, a little drunk perhaps. Then she walked away.

He remembers watching her move across the parking lot and thinking she was an impressive woman when the electricity of anger was in her veins. He remembers she had the light of ambition and distance in her eyes. He remembers a powerful thrill.

Now Eddie Frank realizes he is back at his own street. He staples his last sign to a telephone pole and heads for home. Matthew Ernest is waiting for him on the patio. With Mateo at his side, he is drinking his first cup of coffee and smoking his first cigarette of the day. Eddie Frank likes this scene: his two best friends sitting together groggily on his own back porch in the early morning hours of a day that holds the promise of diversion and excitement and perhaps even adventure, of money to be made and manly labor to be done in a spirit of fellowship.

He says brightly, "Morning, Matthew Earnest."

"Morning, Eddie Frank," the other returns, trying to match the brightness, but then he goes into a coughing fit so deep and profound that Eddie Frank has to slap him on the back.

By nine o'clock it's raining and business is rotten. By ten o'clock Eddie Frank is thinking seriously about giving it up and hauling all the junk to the Goodwill store. And how will they work on the fence if it's raining? He sees doom in everything.

Even in Matthew Ernest, who is sitting in an old easy chair and reading a book Marcia came across called *Co-Ediquette*. It's a book from back around the turn of the century that was written to advise young girls how to comport themselves when they went to college. He can't believe that Matthew Ernest is so interested in it. Because he himself is bored. He hasn't made even fifty dollars and hasn't had a customer in well over an hour.

"So what's that stupid book about?" he wants to know.

"Mainly it's telling 'em to keep their knees together."

"That's wise advice," he says with disagreeable volume.

"What's wrong with you?"

"Look around."

They look around and what they see gets their attention and keeps it. A beautiful woman is walking up the driveway under an umbrella. She has black hair and a warm round face and long slender legs. Turns out Eddie Frank knows her. Sort of. She is the divorced daughter of an old man, a friend of Eddie Frank who lives around the corner. She often visits her father on the weekends and he has met her there before. She is an admirable woman with a gentle manner and he has fantasized about her in the past. When she reaches the garage she smiles in such a way that the two men jump to their feet.

She says, "Hi, Eddie."

But it's to Matthew Ernest she turns in her time of need. She has picked up several items—a set of Scottie dog bookends, a lamp without a shade, a small table that needs refinishing—and it's all about to spill. Matthew Earnest leaps to her aid.

"What are you gonna do with all this stuff?" he asks.

"It's for my father," she says in a low voice, and Eddie Frank nods his head anticipating her answer. He knows the story. "He's retired now and fixing up things keeps him busy. He has a workshop. The bookends are for me."

"Do you have a Scottie dog?"

She nods and smiles.

"What a coincidence. I grew up with a Scottie."

Eddie Frank flinches at this line, for he knows it was not a Scottie that Matthew Ernest grew up with; it was a red dachshund.

The two talk as she looks over Eddie Frank's items. And then she quits looking over his items. She seems very interested in Matthew Ernest, and Eddie Frank can see why. He happens to know that she is a lonely woman and devoted to her father. She's shy too. But Matthew Ernest has a certain way with women, always has. Now Matthew Ernest is telling her about his being a writer and how he lives alone in a remote cabin and how he has committed his life to literature, and he makes it all sound as if he's a martyr for art. Then come the formal introductions.

"Oh! Are you two related?" she asks.

Eddie Frank says, "Yeah he's my son," and Matthew Ernest gives him a hard glare. The woman just looks confused.

Her name is Sandra Boone. Used to be Grapestone but since her divorce she has gone back to her father's name. Matthew Ernest seizes this opening and tells her he is alone too. Now she's even more interested. Eddie Frank sees love blossoming right there in his cluttered garage and he's deeply envious.

But he has new customers, two middle-aged housewives. And now here's a young couple. They come into the garage under umbrellas or pieces of newspaper and he has to keep an eye on them, take their money, find bags for their items. Still he tries to listen to Matthew Ernest and Sandra Boone. They have taken a seat on a picnic bench. For almost an hour they talk until Matthew Ernest has somehow convinced her to go out with him that evening.

"Suppose the three of us make a night of it?" Matthew Ernest says, glancing at Eddie Frank, who shrugs and nods his head yes despite the murmured warnings of his wiser angels.

She's ready to pay but Eddie Frank can't see taking money from Sandra Boone. She says, "Oh thank you, Eddie." His eyes almost tear up at the sound of her gentle voice speaking his name and the sight of her friendly smile, and he regrets very much being married, even to Marcia. He thinks also that Matthew Ernest is not the right man for her.

Watching her walk away, Eddie Frank says to Matthew Ernest without looking at him, "You be good to her, you hear me."

"It's a little early for that kind of warning, isn't it?"

"Maybe," he says.

Then he busies himself taking what remains of his junk off the tables and dropping it all into boxes. He and Matthew Ernest are quiet with each other as they heft the boxes into the truck and then drive to the Goodwill store. They unload the stuff at the back dock, and as they pull away Eddie Frank feels a mixture of loss and relief, of sadness and new freedom.

Eddie Frank has been thinking too much again, and he's dirty and tired. It quit raining just after lunch, so he and Matthew Ernest have been ripping off four-foot slats and banging up six-footers all afternoon. There is an unruly pile of lumber in the middle of the yard. He hadn't thought of that: what's he going to do with the old wood? Whenever he looks at it he sighs over this new affliction and wants to kick Mateo for getting him into this.

And he misses Marcia. Everything seems unnatural without her. It's a loneliness hardened by the cruelties she has committed against him lately. A dozen times he has replayed in his mind the scene in which she told him she didn't like his name.

"I mean, I don't want to hurt your feelings or anything," she said. "But Eddie's just kind of dumb, it's a kid's name."

"But it's my name," he said.

"Well that's not my fault."

"Well it's not mine either."

"But you can do something about it," she said.

He bangs up the next slat and then steps back panting for air. *But you can do something about it,* he mouths, wagging his head, mocking her. He thinks he is speaking only in his mind but apparently something has slipped out.

Matthew Ernest says, "What was that?"

"Nothing."

"Hey, look now, something's up, you've been talking to yourself all afternoon. Did I piss you off somehow, Eddie Frank?"

"Naw. It's this name bullshit," he says without thinking.

Matthew Ernest just looks at him. His hair, his face, his beard, his clothes—all soaked with sweat. He smiles. It's a teasing smile full of friendly contempt and a wry kind of pleasure. Exhausted he sits on the grass cross-legged and lights up a cigarette. Mateo slinks over and gently falls in his lap.

"I've changed my mind," says Eddie Frank. "I ain't no Frank and I sure as hell ain't no Eddie Frank. My name's Eddie."

"Yeah I know."

"And that's what I want to go by."

"Fine."

"And you're Matt."

"I sure am."

"So it's settled?"

"On this end it is."

"All right then." He shakes the hammer once for emphasis.

Matt says, "Eddie's a fine name, I've always liked it."

"You're damn right it is."

"Damn right."

"Goddamn right."

Mateo, confused and excited by the banter, suddenly lets out a weak bark and thumps his tail, gazing up, hoping for reassurance. Matt strokes his head and says, "It's okay, we ain't arguing." Eddie and Matt look at each other for a long moment and some kind of understanding passes between them.

Eddie says, "Hand me some nails, would you."

"Yessir."

They make one last trip to Builders Square just at closing time and it's a small load they bring home. They have a beer on the patio to celebrate and to cool off and then Matt goes into the house to call Sandra Boone. After a few minutes he returns. His face is troubled but he seems to find the trouble amusing.

"Sandra wants to bring along a friend."

"What kind of friend?"

"Her name's Joan."

Eddie snorts a laugh. "I'm a married man."

"It ain't no date or anything."

He sits still a moment, trying to think of something else to say. He knows there is only one thing to say and he knows they both need to hear it. Onward; march onward. Matt would only laugh at such a phrase so he nods his head yes without speaking.

Alone then Edward Mansfield steps into the yard and takes a good look at his new fence. There is the pile of old lumber to deal with but he decides then and there to cut it up in the fall for firewood. Mateo is sniffing around the hot tub; as he approaches, shooing away the dog, he too smells the faint stench of that drowned squirrel. He reaches into the scum and lifts the carcass out by its tail, marches to the trash can on the side of the house and drops it in. Such a simple thing.

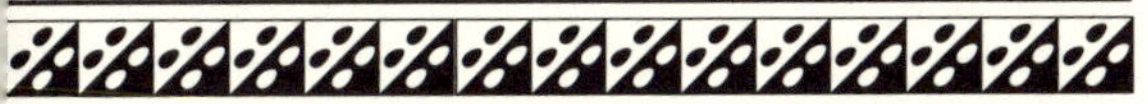

The Solitary Heart

1.

The widower Beamus Hardcastle hung up the phone one day in his hot, dry, dusty living room, parted the billowing lace curtains that his wife had made by hand, looked out at the springtime desert and said with a certain inflection, "Well, shit."

He had to go see those people, the Krafts. It had been the woman's brother on the phone and with bad news again. He hated to do it, there was something about the people that he just didn't care for, but it appeared he had no choice. Somebody had to tell them. After grumbling about it for half an hour over two bowls of lunchtime Corn Flakes, he went outside and hefted his thin tired angular old body into his pickup truck.

Long in retirement Hardcastle still ranched in a small way and tended his laundromat near the college down in Alpine, and he was the Kraft's landlord and closest neighbor at two miles distant. For over a year he had been renting to them the place where he was born, the house in which his parents had lived for almost fifty years. He loved the old house but it had become a burden to Hardcastle and his sister the past few years and he wanted to unload it. The people had promised to buy the house and the five acres he had set aside with it, though no formal offer had been made, and lately they shied from the topic on his brief visits to the porch for the rent check and once to repair the water pump.

In a few words, the people were "pretty goddamn strange." She seemed to think she was an Indian squaw, wearing leather moccasins and headbands and feathers even down in town. And the man more often than not simply stared at him from under his long yellow hair whenever Hardcastle asked him a question; it was as if their isolation up there in the hills had taken the man's voice right out of his body. More than once Hardcastle had heard weird chanting-like music coming from the house when he approached. And smelled unusual odors, like incense, he assumed. Hardcastle's tenants had turned out to be not at all what he had expected: she was a librarian at the college, or had been.

On top of it all there was that contentious half-coyote the people had raised from a pup and kept like any other dog. To Hardcastle, who had considered himself a cattleman even before he was old enough to drive, there was something immoral about anyone who didn't eradicate a coyote at the slightest opportunity. They called him Wolf and the name fit: a good watchdog, except it never barked, which made it all the more sinister and suspect.

The animal rose from the porch when Hardcastle pulled up to the yard, and he saw the Krafts' old rusty pickup. The truck around back meant someone must be home. It usually did at least.

Hardcastle called toward the house: "Hello inside." He noticed his mother's yellow rose bushes going wild up the south wall of yellow stone and a window screen lying on the parched yellow ground. There was other junk in the yard. If he hadn't known better he would have thought the place abandoned. It had been months since he'd seen the inside of the house, and he fully expected to find it an abject mess. He considered asking them to vacate before the locals started to talk even more than they already were or he found out these people were dope smugglers.

He called toward the house again; no one answered so he got out and walked around to the back. The coydog followed him along the yard's picket fence, growling at him, sniffing at him through the pickets. "Beat it!" he said. As he passed through the back-gate opening he kicked at the dog once which sent him scurrying out into the weeds and prickly pear; soon he was back, growling.

Hardcastle knocked on the screen but again no one answered. He stood there on the deep back porch, his hand on their old green washing machine, hoping the Krafts were gone somewhere, hoping he could postpone his errand. At least for a few hours. The wind coming off the knoll from the southwest carried with it the scents of spring, of cactus and wildflowers and West Texas dust, nice smells, familiar smells. Nothing human though. Maybe they were hiding from him, watching him from some hidden spot among the yellow rocks or the green mesquites, afraid for some reason to come and face him, or laughing into their fists.

He was about to leave when way up at the top of the knoll he saw a human form moving around, bending, moving around some more. It looked like the woman. He stepped off the porch into the sunshine, pushed up his eyeglasses, tilted back his Stetson and intensified his gaze: looked like she was picking wildflowers.

She turned. He saw a huge bunch of flowers in her hand. And it was then that he noticed she was naked to the waist.

"Lordy," he said. He held his breath as she stepped from behind a low boulder, showing her slender legs now too.

Hardcastle glanced around to see if anyone was watching him and passing judgment; there was her husband to consider. He saw no one, just as before; all the evidence indicated he and the woman were alone together. So he indulged himself, squinting and blinking to get her into focus. It had been many years since he had seen a young woman's breasts on anything but the pages of a magazine, and these two were awfully far away for his weak old eyes. He wished he had his hunting binoculars. No matter; blurry though it was, the scene did more to charge up his atrophied urges than anything he'd come across in years. She was wearing only underwear—purple underwear, it appeared—and twice when she bent to pick a flower he got a view similar to the one a bull gets when he's headed off to mount a cow across a pasture. At these moments Hardcastle's lust throbbed painfully in his crotch and his boots stirred in the dust. But then she would stand and walk a ways, moving along a barren trail, holding the bouquet of flowers against her belly, looking down, her dark hair falling across her white shoulders and the image would change to something sweet and endearing as if she were a well-endowed child playing in a field . . . and he felt ashamed of himself.

He didn't know quite what to do but figured this had gone on long enough. He decided to call out to get her attention and then he'd make a big show of not looking as she came down the hill. Turned out neither was necessary. She must have seen him at last for she stopped what she was doing, shaded her eyes with one hand and waved to Hardcastle with the other. And she did it without even trying to cover herself. Just then, off to his right, Hardcastle heard the screen door slam out at the old foreman's house which hadn't been used in years. Standing on the stoop was the husband. He seemed preoccupied with something. Hardcastle almost jumped out of his skin trying to get through the gate and up the long path before the man could see what he'd been up to.

Kraft was holding some kind of pot in his hands and blinking in the deluge of afternoon sunlight. His voice was very soft with little inflection when he said, "Hello, Mr. H." He too was naked to the waist and with no shoes on his feet but at least he had on jeans, torn at the knees and sort of rusty-looking. Streamers of sweat glistened on his brown blond-bearded face and his arms were crusted to the elbows with a flaky gray mud. He looked at Hardcastle as if he hadn't seen another human being in a long time and expected this one to do something entertaining.

"Y'all gonna have to get yourselves a telephone," Hardcastle said more loudly and with more jocularity than was necessary. But then bluster was his way with people. With bluster and a little business sense he had gotten along pretty well in life. It didn't seem to be working this time—it rarely did with these people— and he laughed uneasily under the husband's innocent gaze.

"Don't y'all believe in progress?" he tried again in the same blustery tone, but the man just stared at him with the same expectant face. It was like trying to talk to a child. Even his eyes had a childlike innocence and penetration about them.

Hardcastle gave up and attempted a new tack; he spoke to him as he would to a child: "You see, son, I've got a message for your wife. An important one. Is she here by any chance?"

Kraft stared at him for so long that Hardcastle thought perhaps he wasn't going to answer. He began to wonder if there was something wrong with himself, spittle hanging from his mouth or a new wart growing on his nose. He was ready to ask again when the man sort of came to himself and said, "Uh yeah, right, Mr. H. Sorry, I had something on my mind. You wanted Alice?"

"That's right, son."

Kraft said that she had left a while ago, gone to the house, but he had seen her pass by shortly thereafter and he thought she was out picking flowers or maybe she was robbing from the honey bees. "We've got a hive up in the hills now," he said. And then he smiled to himself and went back inside the house.

Hardcastle stepped back, glanced up the knoll and saw the woman was coming toward him, her naked breasts jouncing grandly as she made her way down the trail. He didn't want to be caught alone with her so he quickly invited himself in and followed the husband through the door, removing his Stetson and catching the screen before it hit the jamb. What he saw amazed him.

The inside, nothing more than a large room, was neat and tidy as a hospital though a little dusty and very warm. All the woodwork and cabinets and fixtures were in good repair and the room was freshly painted. It smelled nicely of the paint and of something else, an earthy smell. One of the walls was covered over with pictures, each one framed and carefully arranged from ceiling to floor. The other long wall was rack upon rack of unfinished pottery, some pieces covered in plastic, and each one was accompanied by a tag stuck to the front of the shelf below it. Lined up neatly on the floor were a dozen or more white buckets of glaze. In the center sat a muddy potter's wheel with a smooth lump of clay on top and just beside it squatted the large octagonal kiln, its top propped open, the source of the room's uncomfortable heat. In one far corner was the kitchen, in perfect empty order save a plastic bucket in the sink and a few dishes in the drainer. In the other corner was a narrow bed made up like an army cot and a small dresser. It looked like the man not only worked here but lived here, lived here quite comfortably.

"My word!" said Hardcastle. "Y'all've really fixed this place up. What are you, an artist or something?"

The husband nodded and shrugged in a noncommittal way and said "sort of" and then smiled at Hardcastle from where he stood behind his kitchen table. He asked Hardcastle if he cared for something cool to drink and Hardcastle said no thank you, not right now, just as the woman entered by the door along with the panting coyote who settled itself calmly at the husband's feet.

Her hands were full of bluebonnets and yellow coreopsis and red Indian blanket, and she was dressed now in a white tee shirt and a faded denim skirt. Still the shape of her breasts seemed to jump out at the old man, so he avoided looking at her below the neck. The woman appeared prettier than he remembered, healthier somehow with more weight and breadth and texture in her olive-colored face, and she greeted him as a friend. With the gaze from her caramel eyes fixed on him pointedly, she apologized for the warmth of the room and went on to explain that on days when James was firing in the kiln they had to take extreme measures to keep cool. From a kitchen cabinet she removed a jelly jar, filled it with water and arranged the flowers in it.

"Mr. H, the wildflowers are coming up beautiful this year," she said. "Why don't you take these on home with you. We'll just drain the water before you leave and you can fill it up again."

Hardcastle was so taken by the offer that he accepted the glass of flowers with several thank yous and awkward bows and then the woman asked him what they could do for him. She said with a smile that she hoped they hadn't somehow let the first of the month slip by unnoticed.

"No, ma'am, no, it's nothing like that."

James said, "He has a phone message for you."

"Oh, I see," she said.

"It's from your brother, ma'am. Bad news I'm afraid."

Alice's father had died. Like bookends loosely holding up the fifteen months they had been back in Texas this matched news they had received in March of the year before. That time it was her mother who had died.

"Your brother said he was already in Houston and that the funeral was in two days, on Friday," said Hardcastle. "He left a number for you to call. You can use my phone if you'd like."

Hardcastle noticed absolutely no difference in the woman's face or manner after receiving the news of her father's death. She acted as if she had fully expected him to say exactly what he had said and that it didn't matter to her one way or the other. He even felt a little foolish acting so pious and concerned as he went through the things her brother had told him on the phone, the particulars of how and when and where and what. When he had finished she thanked him for coming over to tell them and then she said the most incredible thing, given the circumstances:

"Is your house, this house, still for sale, Mr. Hardcastle?"

Glancing at the husband Hardcastle coughed once and stuttered a moment before saying, "Well, sure, yes ma'am."

"And you're asking?"

"Forty-five thousand, just as before."

"Would you take forty thousand cash?" she said and then glanced herself at the husband who affirmed the offer with a nod.

Hardcastle laughed strangely and looked again at the husband who sat at the table waiting for him to answer. "Well, yes, ma'am, I guess so," he said to relieve the pressure. "But there's no hurry about anything like that. I mean you got other things to worry over just now and I'm not going to sell it out from under you or anything."

"Would you have the papers drawn up?"

"Well . . . well sure, yes ma'am, but there's no rush."

"You're right," she said. "At your convenience."

Hardcastle liked a woman who could take care of business so easily but he was glad when she shifted her attention. She and the husband began to talk lowly between themselves, something about dates and savings accounts, and this too astonished him, how they could seemingly ignore the emotional aspect of death. He stood there staring at the woman, holding his flowers in his hands, listening but not really listening and as he did a new and troubling thought began to prick his mind. He had the feeling he had been taken advantage of somehow. It had to do with numbers. Forty-three thousand had always been his mental minimum price for the house yet he had just agreed to something else. And then he saw what she had done, that she had seized an opportunity and used his delicate feelings toward her just then to negate the possibility of negotiation—a tactic he himself had used a number of times—and suddenly his heart lifted itself to the platform of admiration.

The two had quit talking. There was a strained silence before the woman said, "Well thank you again, Mr. Hardcastle," and he took it to mean she wanted him to leave. The husband got up and shook his hand as if to seal a pact and then returned to his seat at the table without saying a word. She walked out with him and as they approached his truck it struck him that he had apparently just sold his family's home place and he might never have a chance to see the inside again. So he asked her if she would mind letting him take a quick peek for old time's sake and she said, smiling, "Certainly not."

They walked through weeds to the dilapidated porch where he had played as a child, and she opened the weathered old door. He stepped inside expecting the worst. But this too amazed him.

It was beautiful inside. All of the woodwork and walls and cabinets had been redone and the old wood floors glistened with varnish.

There wasn't a curtain on any window and the furniture was very plain, very old, very sparse, but pictures covered the walls and on each floor rested a lovely rug of an intricate design, the kind you see in museums. In the front bedroom was a gigantic loom interlaced with gray yarn and a worktable covered with beads and tools. And in the back room he found a bed almost identical to the one in the husband's place, simple and narrow like a cot. Above the bed hung a huge painting. It was abstract but he assumed it was of a wolf or maybe their own coyote.

She saw him staring at it and told him they had commissioned the painting by an emerging artist in New Mexico and that it was called "The Essence." Again he exclaimed the way they had "fixed up the place," saying it made him feel good to think of it "pretty like this." She told him that her husband was something of a carpenter and had done the work all by himself.

"Well I'll be damned," he said and please excuse my French. And he asked if she too were an artist of some kind like her husband. She nodded serenely and smiled with a little doubt.

"I'll be damned," he said in the kitchen, drinking a glass of water, listening to the agreeable young woman go on talking about the house and their life in it. It was cool in the kitchen and dark and somehow remote from the world, and he could faintly smell the woman's body and her clothing when she crossed her arms or moved her hips against the remodeled counter. He found himself recalling the sight of her earlier nakedness and wishing that he could see it again, now, up close. And from deep in his aged loins an ancient and nearly forgotten message stirred his imagination. What if, he kept thinking, what if? So his imagination sent back a message to his loins as a scene of the young woman naked and smiling for him lodged itself in his mind. This went on until he was actually leaning forward, about to put out his lips to kiss her, when he realized she had stopped talking and was looking at him now in a curious way.

"So it's a fact then. You're not at the college anymore?"

She shook her head no and smiled and he said, because he couldn't think of anything else: "I'll be damned."

Then there was a long silence and he knew what it meant.

On the porch he told her he was awful sorry about her daddy and to let him know if there was anything he could do. She walked him to his truck and said thank you again in the nicest possible way and patted his arm through the window and told him like a sister to look after himself. They were going to be neighbors for a long time to come after all, and maybe it was time they got to know each other better. Why sure, he said and fumbled to start the truck. Then she waved goodbye to him in big sweeping strokes and stood out front watching him drive away, watching till he was out of sight as if perhaps she really did care for him.

About halfway home he stopped the truck at a turnout with a particularly pretty view. It was a place he used to bring his wife when they were first married and still sparking over each other, and he hadn't stopped here in many years. You could see the town below and the desert shimmering beautifully around it and beyond it forever. He sat there smelling his flowers, thinking of the young woman in her time of trouble and then thinking of the young woman sleeping alone in the old house in her narrow bed, and for just a moment he had the feeling he had fallen in love with her. Something in his narrow chest swelled and surged without his control; his lips moved as if trying to form a word, and he had to blink his eyes several times. Who's to say it couldn't happen? Who would deny two lonely people their time together if they needed each other? Here she is now without any family to speak of and with a husband who keeps himself apart like that. It's not right, he thought and absently sniffed his flowers. Soon a cloud passed below the sun and its shadow dulled the beautiful scene before him and the feeling in his chest inexplicably faded. He saw with fresh eyes what was out there, nothing but a harsh desert, an arid howling empty place upon the earth.

"You old fool," he said to himself and then tossed the flowers out the window.

At the house Hardcastle immediately called his sister to let her know that he had sold Mama's house for cash money and to let her know also what all he had found out about those people that everybody had thought so strange since they came to Alpine. His sister Abilene Jones, who had buried three husbands and lived in an apartment down in town, said she'd believe it about the house when he had the money in his hands. Then Abilene called her cousin Odessa and told her all about it and Odessa called Sister Grace from the Church of Christ and told her about it. And then other calls were made and before nightfall everybody in town who mattered knew that those people up in the hills near Beamus went around the house naked and even outside in plain view . . . but . . . and now get this! Beamus says they don't sleep together.

2.

Being a Wednesday it was James's turn to prepare supper. He still was not much of a cook but he did the best he could that evening and put together two plates of enchiladas verdes with beans and rice and corn tortillas and then placed them on the kitchen table in his studio. From his little refrigerator he took the gallon bottle of Chablis that he had been drinking from for a week and set it on the table too next to the vase of Indian blankets which Alice had returned to pick when Hardcastle left that afternoon. The flowers and the wine bottle and the steaming plates of food atop the red-checked place mats created a festive air. He moved the flowers so they were squarely in the center of the table and then wiped his sweating face with a dishtowel.

The kiln had been down for several hours now; still it was an incredibly warm spring evening, especially for April, though very dry and breezy. In defense against it he was wearing only sandals and a pair of long white boxer shorts which Alice had bought for him at the Army surplus store in Alpine. He considered changing into something else or at least putting on a shirt but he knew Alice wouldn't care, wouldn't even notice and he would just have to strip it off later.

James scrutinized the table; everything was ready, it appeared, so he went to the door, stepped outside and rang the rusty cowbell that hung by a chain from the eaves.

Presently Alice and Wolf appeared on the back porch of the house fifty yards away and started up the narrow path toward him. His place was slightly higher than the house, and he looked down on them, watching them as they passed through the opening in the picket fence and then as they walked among the prickly pear and the cholla and underneath their only paloverde, blooming yellow. They were pretty to watch (Wolf sprang at her side, teasing her hand) in the gentle dusk light that follows the glorious sunsets in that part of the country. And he noticed again how her body had filled out with its own blooming grace, more womanly and more forgiving. She moved with a fluid and languid sort of grace which she had never exhibited in the early years when they were trying to make careers in the city . . . and a family. And then there was the accident on that distant island in that distant lake that caused her to lose the child and caused them to lose forever the chance to have another. It had changed her in ways neither could understand, ways mysterious and monumental. And it had changed him of course. Looking at her, seeing Wolf, always reminded him of how the simple travesties are usually the ones that lead to the greatest and most terrible deviations of human life. Tonight the stars themselves seemed to be condemning him.

He heard her sandals slapping against her heels; otherwise she was wearing only underwear again and her breasts swayed in her rhythm as if they were the engines that powered it all. When she got close enough for the weak lantern light inside the studio to reach her he saw that she had adorned herself simply this night: a single eagle's feather hung from her hair, brushing her bare shoulder, and, yes, she had painted up her eyes. The scar on her belly showed hardly at all. She cocked her head and smiled.

"Come in," he said.

He turned off the kerosene lantern and lit a candle for the table. The place had electricity but it was used only for the refrigerators and to heat the kiln. As usual Alice awaited her invitation; quickly James pulled out her chair and motioned for her to sit in her usual place at the small unpainted table. There was a moment of silence and of probing looks meant to ask if all was well. The faces, hers light and clean, his dark and bearded, to each said yes, said as well as can be expected and thanks for asking, said also please let's move beyond that now.

"Welcome," said James, raising a toast.

They ate eagerly and quickly, sipping wine, saying very little beyond a few teasing comments on the tastiness of the food and how much better James was getting as a cook. He gave all the credit to the Mexican cookbook she had given him for his birthday. The wine bottle sat mute and empty by the time the last forkful of rice was lifted to Alice's mouth and their glassy eyes were blazing and lively in the candlelight. For dessert they had peach ice cream which James had cranked himself in an old wooden bucket. Then he smoked his pipe as she tried to teach Wolf to respond to the command "speak, speak." She gave up when all he did was cock his head in confusion.

"Care for some stargazing?" she said.

Outside in the hammock they lay side by side picking out constellations and marveling as usual at the number of shooting stars in the West Texas sky. Not a sound could be heard but the remote racket of the insects. They talked briefly about some new pieces she had uncrated that morning at the art gallery down in Alpine where she worked part-time with the title "assistant manager." James displayed his pottery there and Alice had sold a few pieces of jewelry. Her weaving wasn't mature enough yet to sell though often the wee hours found her bent into the lantern light in her front-room workshop as she labored to improve.

They did not talk about the death of her father. That had all been consigned to the realm of old business long ago, and Alice had settled in her conscience the remaining details while working at her loom that afternoon. Her brother Bobby, a career soldier stationed at that time in Georgia, would call again in a few days, and if she chose to call him back she would try to sooth and pacify him. They would finish up whatever arrangements needed finishing up and then she would more than likely never speak to him again. Checks for her share of the inheritance would arrive in time at the post office and that would be that. She felt somehow free for the first time in her life.

She had no intention of going to the funeral. Her family had for years been a part of someone else's life, not hers. She had attended her mother's funeral after driving a long hard day in the truck with one idea in mind: to see her father and brother one last time. She had refused to look at her pasty-skinned mother in her casket and sat without emotion through the graveside service. Humid Houston was so lush and green compared to arid Alpine that she had passed the ordeal staring first at one and then another of the many beds of enormous pink azaleas which were blooming hotly in the cemetery at that time.

On that last visit her brother had nothing to say to her and her father had told Alice all about his money and his will, where certain keys and important papers were hidden. He said that for years, without mentioning it to her mother, he had been putting away some each month in savings accounts and investing in insurance policies so that when he died she and James, and Bobby and his wife, would not have to struggle the way their parents had. He figured it was all worth about fifty thousand each, and of course there was the house which they could sell. That night she slept in her white-painted childhood bed for the last time, and in the morning she couldn't wait to get on the road home.

Now, at home, the mosquitoes began to pester and the night chilled and Alice said, "Why don't we go inside tonight . . . my place." James followed her down the path.

In her new freedom she made love with even more zeal than usual of late. The narrow bed under the huge painting of the wolf creaked and strained beneath them in the eerie light of a gibbous moon, a light that seemed to emanate from the room itself. She enjoyed James's constant efforts to find new approaches to their love-making, and at one point they broke into friendly laughter, finding themselves sprawled upon the hard wooden floor. They scrambled back onto the bed like otters at play in a stream.

It thrilled her when they were like this. Everything about it was more profound on such nights, the likes of which they had enjoyed only in the past few months, once she had healed completely and their mourning had subsided somewhat. There was nothing to fear anymore, nothing to lose, nothing tangible to hope for in their coupling now and therefore none of the old despair that used to well up afterwards. It was the ultimate act of creation made joyful with abandon by the knowledge that they would never again bring forth the ultimate creation itself.

They lay still and soaked on the soaked sheets, touching along the sides of their bodies, staring at the high ceiling in the large open and eerily white room. The cool breeze from the large windows licked at them. On the verge of sleep they were quiet, breathing quietly now, and they lay this way for a long time until she roused herself and whispered, "Is there anything else I may do for you, my friend?" She saw him smile in the moonlight and shake his head no, and they touched hands, palm to palm, which was their signal. He kissed her hair, lingered a moment and then he slipped on his boxer shorts and his sandals and quietly left the room, muttering only: "'Night, Wolf."

Alone then she watched from her bed as his shadow walked the path through the fence and then disappeared within the deeper shadow beneath the eaves of the other house. His screen door banged and then everything was silent again and she was truly alone. Utterly, absolutely alone in the immensity of the night.

Outside the old moon shone down on the earth like a great torch against darkness and it shone on her too, a solitary part of the earth, and its light, finding her, made her happy. Soon after a little sleep perhaps she would rise and go to her loom where she would pass the lonely hours with hands made busy by the demanding shuttle, the quarrelsome yarn, the ill-tempered and biting needle . . . but not just yet. There was this happiness, this quiet and this stillness to revel in, the real warp and woof of her life, and who would deny her such a simple indulgence? Who indeed would not encourage her to seize what was rightfully hers?

Burn on, old moon, she thought, burn on; I'll be only a short while without you.

Her Name Was

Sheila Wells

The widow called on a Friday afternoon while Sheila and I were in the kitchen sharing some of her butter rolls and grind-your-own coffee.

"Is your offer still good?" she asked over a bad connection.

"Yes ma'am," I said. "As far as I know."

"Two fifty?"

"Is that what I offered?"

I looked at Sheila and shrugged my shoulders and she smiled at me with her round cheeks as she took up a quarter and started scratching at the five dollars worth of lottery tickets she'd picked up at the Stop 'N Go.

"Yes. That was your bid," said the woman on the phone, and I could tell by her voice that it was a disappointment to her to have to take so little and that she was trying hard to sound firm so I wouldn't put a move on to gyp her down even more, as she was in a bind. And she sounded a little anxious too, as anyone might. So she said again, "You offered two hundred and fifty dollars for everything in my shed."

"Well ma'am," I said, "if that's what I offered then that's what it'll be."

"Two fifty?"

"Two fifty."

"It's agreed?"

"On this end it is."

"Good," she said and let out a sigh. Then she gave me a little laugh full of relief. "I've been so worried about this," she said. "It's been almost three months, you know."

"Well you can quit worrying now," I said. "Don't worry about anything. We'll come tomorrow and clear everything out."

"But when?" she wanted to know.

"When do you get up?"

"Oh I'll be up," she said.

"Well ma'am. . . ." I said, but then I caught myself. "Ma'am," I said, "what was your name again? I'm sorry but I'm not very good with names."

She gave another laugh and apologized two or three times saying how rude it was of her that she hadn't given me her name and to please excuse her but she wasn't her old self these days. I said not to worry, I understood, and I laughed some myself.

So the first tension was gone then.

"Mulhollen's my name," she said. "Mrs. John H. Mulhollen. Margaret, if you'd like."

"Mulhollen," I said and wrote it down on my pad.

"That's right."

"Margaret," I said and wrote that down too.

"That's right."

"I'm not very good with names, you see."

"I understand."

"And what was the address again?"

"Two-sixty-two First Archer Lane," she said, and it was then for the first time that I fully remembered the widow and her shed and the bid I had given her to buy the junk inside.

"Well ma'am, as I was saying, you get up in the morning and have yourself a nice breakfast and read the newspaper and by the time you're finished we'll be there with the truck and a check."

"Two fifty, right?"

"That's right."

"Doesn't hardly seem enough," she said. "It was everything he cherished, you know. His tools and his hobbies and . . . .and just everything. His whole life, you could say, at least toward the end. It was all left behind in that shed out there. It just doesn't seem enough, but no one else would offer even what you offered. I've been advertising off and on for three months."

"Yes ma'am."

I looked at Sheila again while the widow was talking, and she grinned and shrugged, holding up the lottery tickets, shaking them as if they were some worthless dead thing that now had a smell and then I watched as she threw them in the trash can. She tried to make me laugh by mouthing talk, talk, talk and pointing at the phone, so I turned away and went back to business.

"I just don't understand it," the widow was saying. "You would think it was worth more than two hundred and fifty dollars. A man's whole life, I mean. You know."

"Yes ma'am," I said. "I can see your point, I sure can. But times are bad just now. Not much money to spread around."

"I guess you're right, Mr. Wells," she said. "Texas is suffering, I know."

"Yes ma'am."

"Well. . . . " she said but she didn't go on.

"Like I said now, don't worry. Get up, take it easy, we'll be there early. We'll take care of everything."

"All right, Mr. Wells."

"Goodbye now."

There was a silence on the line that said more was coming.

"Mr. Wells?"

"Yes ma'am?"

"Will it take you long?"

"We'll be in and out by lunchtime," I said optimistically. "Two, maybe three trips, I figure."

"That's fine."

"Okay?"

"Yes that's fine."

"Goodbye now, Mrs. Mulhollen."

"Mr. Wells?" the widow asked again.

"Yes ma'am?"

She hesitated for a moment and sighed heavily and then she said, "Mr. Wells, would you mind calling me Margaret?"

Now I hesitated because it sounded important to her for some reason, and I imagined her blushing over it. But this was business after all, so I said, "I'd be glad to, Margaret."

"It's just something I'd appreciate."

"Margaret," I said to seal the pact.

"That's right," she said and sort of laughed again.

"I've always liked the name Margaret," I said and winked at Sheila sitting at our table. "Margaret's a lovely name."

"Well I doubt that," said the lady on the phone, still laughing a bit. "But it's my name at least."

The silence this time said for sure the thing was over, though I can't say that I was glad of it because I was enjoying making her laugh and sigh and telling her not to worry. But I had rolls and coffee getting cold on the table and other things to do.

"Goodbye now, Margaret."

"Oh . . . yes," she said as if I had interrupted her thoughts. "Thank you, Mr. Wells, and I'll see you in the morning."

I gave Sheila a quick skeptical glance which met the same kind of glance coming back at me, and we smiled in that faint way of people who know each other well enough to be still at times. Her face was full of questions the answers to which she assumed she already knew, or knew well enough, which meant they would wait, and so I sat down at the table again and finished my butter roll and drank my coffee while she got up to do the dishes. She was working four tens at that time which gave her a three-day weekend and time to help me out when I needed her. It was not a happy business I was in then, and I'm glad it didn't last long. Within a year I was called back to the refinery in Houston and quit with buying the left-behind belongings of dead people, quit with the sweltering flea market where I sold the stuff once a month to bring in a little. Sheila paid the bills, but it was good to have some extra coming our way in case one of the boys, pretty much on their own by then, needed our help or we wanted to get out with our camper to the lake for a few days. I didn't like the business but I was good at it.

Sheila was through with giving me time to think and she wanted to be through with the dishes too, so she came over and got mine and gave them a quick scrub.

"Margaret, eh?" she said, lowering herself into the chair across from me, and she grinned at me with her gapped teeth that we'd been planning for years even then to get fixed.

"She's an old gal that lost her husband and needs my services. It'll make us some money, I promise you."

"And she needs my services too?"

"It's a lot. You won't believe what all's in there. Every kind of tool you can imagine, cases of motor oil, model airplanes still in their boxes, eight or ten pairs of brand new leather work gloves, that sort of thing. And the guy bought at least two of each. That shed's crammed to the rafters. It'll probably mean a garage sale on our part too, to get rid of it all."

"Have we got the room out there?"

"I'll straighten up a bit this afternoon. Seems like all I ever do in my life is clean out garages."

"And sheds."

"And sheds."

"What was the darned Margaret stuff?"

Something in the way she said it, as if she were making fun of her perhaps, sullied the nice feeling I had had in doing what the lady had asked of me and calling her Margaret as if we were friends. Sheila made the widow seem for a moment like something pitiful and lonely and distant. Which is how we usually were about my "clients," as I liked to call them, distant and cold and clinical in the way a surgeon must be toward the human specimen lying open on the table before him. It was business after all.

"I don't know really," I said in a moment. "For some reason she wanted me to call her Margaret instead of Mrs. Mulhollen."

"A real chum huh? She must remember you pretty well."

"I was a name and a phone number on a piece of paper, that's all, with two fifty and a dollar sign written at the bottom."

"I can see her reason, I think."

"You can, eh? Let's hear it."

She put on her wise look and shifted in her seat as she lit up a cigarette and then took a deep, heart-thumping drag.

"Wants her own identity back, now he's gone. It's only natural. You read about it all the time in the magazines." Then she smiled in a teasing way and said, "I'll probably do the same thing when you kick off. I'll say, "Call me Sheila please."

"And I guess they'll all do it too, won't they?"

"Sure they will."

"Out of respect for Old Miss Sheila?"

"That's right. Out of respect for Miss Sheila."

"But me? I won't, will I? You wouldn't catch me doing it."

"You speak the truth there, my friend. In fact I can't recall the last time you called me by my name. It's always, 'Hey, Honey,' or 'Hey, Darling,' or 'Hey, you,' or something like it."

"And I have no plans to change either. Even when I'm croaked I'll still just call you My Old Lady from wherever I wind up. And when I'm dead and the guy like me comes to buy all my old tools and junk and what-have-you out there in the garage, I'm gonna whisper down and tell him don't do it. Don't call her Sheila." I was grinning at her now. "Just call her The Old Hag."

"Hah!" she said and slapped the table once lightly.

It was meant as a joke, and she took it as a joke, and we laughed a bit then and glanced at each other from under our eyebrows. Sheila picked at a crumb on the tabletop and shifted her sizable hips in her seat until it was clear the light moment had passed and we had nothing else worth saying to each other. Still we sat there a few minutes, sat there imagining the thing, smiling over it occasionally, postponing whatever else we had to do that day and enjoying the cool of the kitchen, enjoying the warmth of each other's quiet company, which at that time we'd been enjoying more or less regularly for twenty-four years. But Friday, then as now, is a workday all day long. Finally I lifted my long body from the chair I'd been sitting in, and she looked up and followed me with her eyes until at the door to the garage I mumbled, "Guess I better get back to it." She nodded her head then and gazed at me in a simple direct way that said quite matter-of-factly: I love you, Ralph Wells, and I already miss you, and you just better not die on me any time soon.

Family Photos

1. Still Life With Geranium

His mother, who had just come in from the hall, and his father, who had met them outside and ushered them into the house, were kissing each other there in the living room. He hadn't seen them do that in years. Teddy and Mary were making a big noise over it. "Yea," they cried, and, "Happy Thanksgiving."

Speaking to himself because none of them could hear him over the clapping and the boisterous talk, Randy said, "Strong affection, warm attachment, attraction based on sexual desire, a beloved person, a score of zero in tennis. . . ." and he stood in the corner, his hands in his pockets.

But here came Teddy. Three steps and his brother was standing in front of him. He had a funny look on his face as if he were about to ask Randy whether he needed to go to the head.

"You okay?" said Teddy and now here was his mother's face,

beaming, peering over Teddy's shoulder. She must be on tiptoe, Teddy's so tall. Then Teddy stepped aside and here came his mother's arms, up around his neck, pulling him away from the wall, and then here came her face: a kiss on the cheek by his mouth. And as her face moved away Randy smelled the woodsy breath of a cigarette smoker. She seemed so happy she might cry.

"Oh my goodness," she said. "It's so good to have you home. You look good. What're you doing here in the corner, come on over here, we've been looking so forward to having you, come on over here and have a seat." She pulled on his arm and he followed her to the couch as the faces of Teddy and Mary and his father passed by him. She said, "Here, take off your jacket, honey."

A simple "no" came to his mind but he caught himself and said, "Used to express . . . no . . . here, let me express the negative of an alternative choice or possibility." He smiled for his mother. Her face showed confusion at first but then her eyes tightened and her mouth drooped as if he had hurt her feelings.

"What'd you say, dear?" asked his mother. And she patted him on the chest. "Oh never mind. Are you cold? Just keep it on. . . . Hey, Hugh, why don't you turn up the heat? Randy's cold."

She pulled him onto the couch, sitting so close that her hip rested against his thigh. She looked at his face as if she were going to touch it and then looked away and then looked at his face again with a curious twisted smile. She seemed about to say something, her face frozen in a happy expression, but she only sighed and snuggled closer. Straining, she reached up, pulled off his red ball cap and tossed it onto a chair. "There," she said.

Settled now she turned her attention to Teddy and Mary as if she hadn't noticed them before and wanted to make them feel welcome. She said, "Now, you two, how in the dickens are you . . ." and they exchanged the usual pleasantries as Randy toyed with a piece of paper in the pocket of his jacket.

He hadn't been so close to his mother in a long time. She felt soft yet heavy, solid, and he could smell her perfume and hair spray. The smells were strong and tickled his nose and for an instant he remembered himself as a little boy sitting on the toilet lid looking up at his mother as she made herself up for . . . for what? For work? To go out? Did she have a job once? And he remembered the face coming down to kiss him and the mask of makeup and the strange tickling smell of perfume and hair spray and he remembered that he always wanted to reach up and touch his mother's hair then but he never dared do it. He never dared because she would have been so kind, saying, "No, darling, don't muss it, you little sweetie." And she would have squeezed his face between her hands and kissed him on the lips. . . .

Just then his father's voice said, "I set the thermostat on seventy-four, how's that? Seventy-four ought to warm up ole Randy." And his mother: "That's good, that's good." Then to Randy, "Here, get close, I'll warm you up," and she laughed into his face, "You sweet thing," and her arm flew across his chest and gripped his arm, pulling him so close that his shoulders squeezed up high against his jaw. He felt warm.

The others—his father, Teddy, Mary—kept moving through the room. In and out of the dining room or the hall they went and then back to the middle of the room. Each would stop, smiling stupidly, and look down at him and his mother as if to catch whatever they were saying, as if it were very important.

Someone cried, "Look, it's Janet!" And here she was, saying, "Finally, we get to see him." His sister bent low and kissed him on the cheek. She looked pleased. She said, "You've lost weight."

He smiled for her—such a friendly face but that hair!—and his mother said, "We'll fatten him up today. . . . Oh my God, the turkey!" And she took away her arm. The couch gave a sigh as she got up, having trouble, putting a hand on his knee for leverage, then heaving her body forward. She stumbled, caught herself, threw up a hand to the base of her neck, laughed, "That couch is too low." Then: "Hugh, where's the turkey?" Randy watched her go into the kitchen. His father followed and he could hear their voices, low at first, but then loud. They were arguing.

Janet, taking his mother's place on the couch, said, "Well how've you been?" And he saw Teddy's face and Mary's face looking at him, waiting for an answer.

From the kitchen he heard his father's voice, in a stifled hiss: ". . . Would you hold it down, please. . . . "

Randy looked at Janet and shrugged, and shrugged again, then said, "I'm fine." They smiled at him and nodded as if to get him to continue but their eyes kept darting toward the kitchen. They were all silent until Mary said to Janet, "Have you changed your hair?" and Randy let out a quick laugh—of course she'd changed her hair, it was orange—and they all looked at him. His sister grinned for him, the grin they shared as children when an adult had said something stupid.

"Yes," said Janet. "Everyone's doing it."

Mary acted like she wanted to touch Janet's new orange hair but then here came his father, red-faced and sulky. He said, "Look, I'm going to run get some film, anybody want to go?"

"I'll go," said Teddy.

"Me too," said Mary.

"How about you, Buddy, want to go?"

And again the faces ogled him. He remembered similar trips in the car, everyone quiet at first and then making worthless conversation, comments about the weather or a piece of property up for sale, and he said, "Bathroom."

He got up, wobbly at first, found his footing, then pushed past them toward the hall.

"Hurry up, we'll wait for you," called his father.

He scuttled down the hall to his parents' bedroom, through the bedroom to their bathroom, stepped in and closed the door.

Randy heard a whisper through the bathroom door: "Why's he been in there so long?" It was Mary, Teddy's wife.

Teddy said, "How should I know?"

"Maybe we should check on him."

"Leave him alone."

Mary knocked on the door.

"Don't!"

"What if he's sick or something?"

Randy suppressed a laugh. He said, "Separated from others, not including anyone or anything else."

"There he goes again with that gibberish," Mary said.

"So what. Let him be. Let's go without him . . . ."

He heard their whispers and footsteps fade away. He smiled to himself in the mirror above the counter, on top of which he had spread all sorts of items from the drawers: his father's safety razor and shaving mug, a comb, his mother's eyelash pinchers and tweezers, an eyebrow pencil, a lipstick, a hair net, a jar of cold cream, and several other less interesting things.

His mood, the touch of agitation, and the smell of the bathroom—sweet here, pungent there—brought on a crowd of associations, all of them from his childhood. Once he was certain Teddy and Mary had left him alone, he scooped the items on the counter top into a pile. He picked up the eyebrow pencil, licked the tip and started applying it to his face. Soon both of his eyebrows were dark and thick. Then he pinched his eyelashes, several times, until, by looking closely, he could see them curled, sticking together in pointed clumps like feather tips on a bird's wing. He put on lipstick, smearing it out past the corners of his mouth, then he dug into one of the drawers until he found two little disks of powder and rouge. He rubbed the rouge into circles on his cheeks and then dusted on the powder. His sparse whiskers made the powder glob up along the edge of his jaw. He ripped a piece of toilet paper from the roller, folded it, placed it between his lips and pressed, leaving a crescent of red on the paper. He stared at himself in the mirror but didn't know who he was looking at. It was no one he'd ever seen before.

He turned on the hot water and soaked his father's shaving brush and whipped up lather in the mug. Slowly, eyeing himself in the mirror, he smoothed on the lather. Half moons of pale rouge now protruded from behind the lather on his upper cheeks.

A noise outside the door sent a panic through his chest as if he were a burglar in his parents' house. He heard a door open and close—perhaps a closet—but whoever it was soon left.

Everything smelled so familiar. He had smelled it all when he was a child and used to watch his parents dress themselves. He remembered the talk that went on as the two of them moved around each other, telling the other to get out of the way or to hurry, and the talk always ended in his being told to move: "You're in the way, son." "Go on, now, sweetie." And when he left he always heard the voices, big sounding then, following him down the hall. With his father's heavy-headed razor he shaved himself, drawing blood only once with a nick on his Adam's apple. Then, the remnants of lather still on his jaw, he smeared cold cream over his face until it formed a greasy pap, and the sharp sweet smells filled his head. He cleaned his face—first with a Kleenex and then with splashes of warm water—and toweled dry. From the left side of the counter he picked up his father's aftershave and slapped a palm's worth on his face. And from the right side he picked up his mother's cologne. He dabbed some behind each ear.

Gazing at his pink face in the mirror, he said quietly, "A male offspring or descendant, Jesus Christ, a person deriving from a particular source, as a country, race or school."

The house was quiet when he left the bathroom and crept through the hall to the living room.

Randy stood in the doorway of the kitchen. His mother was bent over the open oven door. When she stood up he saw that she was doing something to the turkey. Turning, startled, she said, "My God! I didn't see you there," and the long fork flew out of her upthrust hand, clattered into the sink.

Randy didn't say anything. He'd been rather drowsy and listless and preoccupied with his inner life for weeks now and the medication he'd been receiving at the hospital had not yet made much of a difference. It was just as well: he had nothing to say to anyone. Each time he had one of these spells of melancholy the heart cavity in his chest got a little deeper, a little wider, while the opening at the top that led to his mouth got a little smaller, making it even more difficult to talk. And this had been the worst spell yet. What he had feared most about coming home after three weeks on the ward was that his family would somehow pry into the opening and make something come out.

"It'll be a couple of hours yet," she said. "You want something to tide you over?"

He shook his head no. She came up to him as if to kiss him again and he felt the muscles in his shoulders tense.

"My goodness," she said, sniffing the air around him. "You certainly smell nice. What have you got on? And you shaved."

She patted him on the chest, gazing into his face with huge glistening eyes. He smiled for her.

"Come on," she said. "I've been wanting to get you alone."

She led him into the dining room and sat at the table near the trophy case that used to be a china cabinet. His baseball trophies were shadows within the shadows of the case. Randy stood behind a chair. She appeared flustered having to look up at him but then said, "I want to talk to you." He nodded but glanced through the kitchen to the back door preparing an escape route.

"Your father and I have been talking," she said and, looking at her hands, added, as if for herself, "which is odd for us." And looking up again: "And I think we've decided some things."

He cocked his head to show he was listening. "We know you want to be independent, you want an apartment or something when you get out, that's what the doctor said, and we agree. We want you to be on your own. But you should never feel that you can't come here whenever you need to."

His mother looked sad and old. It was the first time he'd ever considered his mother old. The thick makeup did not cover the wrinkles around her eyes and mouth and all of her features, taken together, made her appear tired, resigned to something.

"I'll always be here," she said. "This is our home, your home. . . . I know I'm not supposed to say anything that might upset you and if I do just say so and I'll shut up. But you need to know." Her voice took on the quality of a counselor and her words came more deliberately. "Your father's been having some sort of trouble lately. I don't know if it's work, or if he's sick, or if it's me." She took a deep breath. "He's been so far away, so deep in thought. He's even talked about moving out for a while."

She looked up. "Am I upsetting you, sugar? I don't want to upset you." Randy shook his head, said softly, "Go on," and his mother gave a tiny crooked smile for the spoken words. Reaching up, she touched his hand on the back of the chair.

"You know you were always his favorite—donít tell any of the others that—but you were. You were so small when you were born, and so sickly, and I had my hands full with Teddy and then so soon after you came, here came Janet and you just became your daddy's boy. He took you everywhere and loved you so much. And then when you grew up so strong and quick and smart it just seemed like, somehow, my God, we were blessed. He loved to watch you play ball and, you know, he coached your team that one year."

She cut it off with a little gasp-like sob, as if she wanted to cry but couldn't, or wouldn't. She looked at the table top, at the basket of fruit in the center.

"And then when you went away and didn't come home—she wasn't such a bad girl, she had a good disposition, even though we all knew it would never work for you. Do you see that now, that it would have never worked? I mean she was so much older than you and with the baby and all—well, your father just went kind of crazy. He always wanted so much for you. I think he got mad at you and then when we found you and you looked so, so, sort of beaten up, and you were so quiet, like now, and whenever you looked at us it just felt like you were looking right through us. And he got even madder. He thought you were blaming us for something . . . .Were you blaming us for something?"

Her upturned face was pathetic. He took a step toward the

kitchen, but she reached out and took his hand. The walls of the cavity inside him quivered. She said: "Did she hurt you, darling? Did she hurt you bad? I know how women can be. They catch a man and then hurt him, like they're paying back that one man for every bad thing that's ever happened to them? They cut the man out and make him feel cold. Is that what happened? Why don't you say anything? Why won't you talk to us?" He tried to pull his hand free.

She said, "I'm sorry, I'll shut up, but I thought you should know that your father loves you, we all love you and want you to come home now . . . for a while. It's time for you to come home now so we can get everything straightened out."

Randy ripped his hand free and started toward the kitchen.

"All we want is for you to say something to us," she said. "Can't you just talk to us? We can work everything out."

He walked through the kitchen to the door and when he glanced back he saw his mother blowing her nose into a Kleenex.

The cool day was like a salve on his skin. The air smelled fresh and lively with wood smoke. He looked up at the chimney and wondered why his father hadn't made a fire. Always before on holidays, when it was cool, the fireplace in the den had been the center of activity from early morning till late at night.

He walked through the yard. The flowerbeds were still brimming with green things but the trees had turned; they were bright with the colors of autumn. On the stone path he came to the bed of geraniums, soft reds and pinks. A fall bloom, he observed, but it won't last with this cool weather.

The inside of the garage was neat and clean. Tools of various kinds hung on the walls. In the back was a big wooden trunk that his father had built to store sporting equipment. Next to it sat a dusty bag of golf clubs and an old pair of water skis. From the box rose the fumes of his past. He found a basketball and a football and his father's faded catcher's mitt. Every summer afternoon when Randy was a boy his father used to catch his pitches. The outside wall of the garage served as backstop.

He picked up the mitt and rifled the box for a hardball. The leather of the ball was yellowish and crisscrossed with scratches. He remembered that he'd been given the ball as a trophy after pitching a one-hit shutout that sent the team to the play-offs his senior year. That was the year he met Jean.

He started popping the ball into the mitt as he went out to the yard. He tossed the ball high above him and leapt to catch it. He threw it onto the roof of the garage and waited for it to roll down. For several minutes he threw the ball onto the garage and caught it, until he was tired. The illness had made him weak. He sat down on the concrete bench near the geraniums.

The blooms were big and whole. He leaned over and plucked one and held it to his nose. It smelled metallic, pungent, musty, not bad, and he slipped the stem behind his ear. He sat there for a long time then until an image of his mother's face formed in his mind. The face caused a pain at the opening to the cavity. He didn't want to feel the pain, but the image had taken over.

The face told him what he had known for a long time—that she was looking for love. She was looking for it in everything and everyone. That's why her face was sad. That's why she could laugh and smile and even joke but still have a sad face. And he knew that she understood nothing. She knew nothing of herself, her children, her husband. He saw that she knew only pain, a specific pain that picked at that place in her chest where her heart should be, but that she knew nothing of her heart. She knew—and he saw it now—she knew only that when she felt the pain she was feeling love. He had felt the same pain for many years, and he knew what it was, for the only time he felt the pain was at those times when he saw or thought of those people he thought he loved. And there was something sickening about it. The pain came when he saw what it was about them that he loved. He could see now something about each of them that made the pain in the cavity in his chest, and he allowed these things to play through his mind. They were some of the same pictures he saw when, in his room at the hospital, the sounds of ambulances coming and going in the night outside, he felt the emptiest.

He lay on the bench and looked up at the soft blue sky.

His mother is laughing at a joke. She has told the joke many times before and she always laughs. They are at a restaurant and everyone else at the table is smiling or making faces, and someone says, "We've heard that a thousand times," and he sees bubbles of spittle at the edges of his mother's mouth. With her napkin she wipes the bubbles away then glances to either side.

The contrail of a jet formed on the sky, way up. He watched it become more distinct, linear, tracking across the great openness; then it disappeared into the glare of the sun.

His father is dressed for work, hurrying about. "Important meeting," he says. It's early morning, all the children are at the breakfast table. His father walks in, smelling of aftershave, leans across the table for his orange juice, and there, in the folds of his fly, under the points of his vest, is a safety pin. Before he leaves he looks down to be sure it's still fastened.

There was something on the wind. Someone was cooking steaks. He heard voices, a conversation, roll by him as if someone had turned up the volume of a radio and then quickly turned it down.

Teddy in a sweatshirt. A touch football game in a neighbor's yard. Teddy is screaming at Randy for doing something stupid. There has been a scuffle, almost a fistfight. Randy sees himself on his knees on the ground, feeling stupid, and Teddy, very angry, almost kicks him. "You ignorant shit," Teddy yells and one of the other boys says, "Yeah, you ignorant shit." Teddy turns on the boy and says, "Shut up or I'll push your nose in."

The contrail appeared on the other side of the sun.

Janet, crying, her face taut and wrinkled and ugly, stained with tears. She's telling their mother something serious between her sobs. The two of them are sitting on her bed. He can see them through the narrow slit of the barely open door. "I told him not to," she says. "I told him I didn't want to. . . .

These images had locked themselves into the cavity. And they churned up waves of other images until something caught and, like a short movie, a series of pictures rolled through his mind.

His father, gray-haired and business-suited, with a woman. He sees them eating together in the restaurant of the old Plaza Hotel near the university. At first he assumes the woman is a client of his father and he almost goes over to greet them. But something makes him stop. They appear so familiar with each other, side by side in a booth, and, for that reason, he takes pains not to let them see him. He makes an excuse to his friends and leaves the restaurant as quickly as possible.

He had tried to forget it, telling himself it must have been business, but there were the wine glasses. The way they held them up, as if toasting each other, intimated a greater closeness, perhaps even love. He had never considered his father a "lady's man." Handsome, yes, perhaps even charming in a rough-hewn way, but always the homebound type. He wanted to laugh at the idea of his father having a mistress. The word itself seemed ridiculous when applied to his father. It seemed ridiculous until the memory of that day juxtaposed itself with the memory of his mother's sad open face. He went searching for that face.

And then he could see the reflection of his mother and a little boy in a shop window. He was the little boy and he had to look up the window to see her face, she was so much taller then. A music store? Yes. There were trumpets and guitars and violins. And then another reflection in the window, a man, a man his mother seemed to know and like. The man bent and shook Randy's hand and patted him on the head. The man and his mother talked for a long time about places and people he knew nothing about. They kept saying, "Remember. . . ." They said it so many times that they forgot about him. They forgot about him and he wandered away, went to the hobby shop across the mall. He sat on the carpeted floor in the back of the store and turned the pages of a book about rockets, toy rockets. Soon his mother was standing above him. She said, "I'm sorry, sweetheart, but the store is closing. Can we come back tomorrow and pick out a rocket?"

Now a stronger picture crowded in, a more recent picture.

His mother in her apron, the apron he and Teddy and Janet gave her when they were children. It must be Christmastime. Dinner is over and the bottle of sherry is on the table. Small stemmed glasses, some still partly filled with the dark wine, stand among the dishes and platters. His mother's eyes are large and shiny, her lips set in a smile, and she has been "chattering about her silly life," as Teddy calls it. "I think I'm tipsy," she says and turns up the glass to finish her sherry as all the children laugh. His father leans over and says something into her ear. Her smile disappears. And, averting his eyes from his mother's face, Randy sees a stain—it must be grease—on the apron's pink heart. She gets up and clears the table. In the kitchen he sees the stain is faded, as if she has tried to rub it out with a damp rag, but he says, "You've stained your apron," and he shows her where. She glances down and says, "Oh that, that's been there for years. It won't come out." She pats him on the chest and quickly goes to the sink, stares into the sink for a long time before she starts rinsing dishes to put in the dishwasher.

He put the catcher's mitt under his head. He had to adjust the flower behind his ear so it wouldn't be crushed. The white smear of the contrail stretched all the way across the sky now.

His mother seemed silly to him sometimes, silly and sad, but then so did his father. The things they did and said, it seemed, were part of a never-ending show in which they had no choice but to perform, their lines and actions written for them by someone who wanted to watch them squirm. They were caricatures, every movement grand, every word fraught with message, every sentence the completion of one begun by the other actor, their eyes always seeking cues, asking, Did I say that right? What now? He couldn't imagine them with separate lives; they were merely Mom and Dad, always together. The word "marriage" even seemed silly in relation to them, as if they had come into the world joined in body and mind and had no distance over which to view themselves as separate. They were an animal with two heads, like something in the circus, the eyes of one always gazing into the distance, the eyes of the other always following the gaze. The earnest, beseeching gaze, like a photo of a soul-warmed couple on a religious calendar. They didn't know they were silly, had no way of knowing. He couldn't imagine his mother ever wanting to know, for fear, the fear of knowing. His father? Maybe. And he wondered, was it his mother's silliness that made him think it possible his father knew another woman, or was it her sadness? Can you hate your own sadness? And can that make you silly? Perhaps she did see her sadness and, hating it, turned away, sought relief.

Perhaps she knew another man? She had once. And a new image came to his mind of his parents with lecherous grins on their faces as they chased each other, on a beach, grabbing and prodding private parts of their bodies. How silly.

He told himself to stop it, turn it off. He thought he should do something to turn it off. But he wasn't sure he wanted to go back inside and he didn't know where else to go. So he lay on the bench and watched a small cloud ease across the sky.

The four of them, his family, are standing in muddy-white water at the edge of a beach. A jetty of jagged rocks angles away behind them. They are a blurred portrait until Randy focuses the camera. Each of them is red from the sun and dressed in a swimsuit. Teddy has a fishing pole over his shoulder and his father is holding a net. None of them likes to be photographed and so they are cutting up. Janet, who comes only to her mother's waist, is making clown faces. Teddy is hopping as if he has springs on his feet. His mother's hands are on her hips and she is talking, trying to calm everyone so the ordeal can be completed. His father suddenly reaches behind the others and loops the net over his mother's head. Randy pushes the button to get the picture. When he takes the camera down he sees his mother, standing apart from the others, struggling with the net and kicking at the water. His father and the children are laughing at her. She frees herself, throws the net down. She slogs out of the water, her head down. She says, "Give me that camera," and he does. She walks back to the water and heaves the camera out into the waves.

Lying there he thought he knew now why he had left college and the house and gone away with Jean to live on her aunt's farm and why, after that had ended, he had come back to the city and worked at a vegetable stand and why he had lived for weeks in a dirty hotel room down the street from the vegetable stand until one day he couldn't get up in the morning and he lay in that bed for three days before the manager told him to leave . . . and the next thing he remembered was the face and white-clad shoulders of a doctor leaning over him and the faces behind the doctor were those of his parents and when he saw the faces he felt the pain in the cavity of his chest and screamed, "Get them out of here!"

Randy stood up from the bench and went into the house. His mother was still at the dining table. She looked around and smiled the smile of someone who wants to hear something sweet and pleasant but fears the sound of something harsh and cruel. He walked up to her, took the geranium from behind his ear and gave it to her. He said, "Here, you wear this. It'll look nice."

She smiled up at him in thanks and tried to put her arms around his waist but he turned and walked away. He went to his bedroom and lay down on his old bed.

2. Secret Exposures

There was a rumble in the attic. The furnace had cycled on. From the vent over the bedroom door blew a gust of warm air. The brown fringe of the bedspread on the top bunk fluttered in the breeze. He lay still on his bed and watched it flutter.

He had dozed for a while, waking, sleeping again. His mother looked in on him once; he had heard the door open and close, as when he was young. Then the others came home. Voices rattled the house, shoes thumped the floor. Now he could tell that someone was in the utility room down the hall: the door to the clothes dryer banged shut and here came the machine's soft rotating purr. His scalp tingled. They were in the hall just outside his room. He heard voices, his parents, whispering, arguing again.

"It might be juicy but you can't stuff a barbecued turkey."

"It's not barbecued, it's smoked."

"Big difference." Her voice boomed.

"Shhh. They'll hear you."

"That's why I wanted a Butterball."

"How was I supposed to know that?"

"I wanted stuffing and gravy, and so will they."

"Then do your own damn shopping from now on."

"Shhh. Bud's trying to sleep."

"Oh."

So it was the turkey. His father had been carrying the brown bag when Randy and Teddy and Mary arrived from the hospital. He had met them outside on the sidewalk—his blue Ford bounced into the driveway just after they parked at the curb—and Randy had thought it odd that his parents had only that morning bought the turkey. He sensed they had been arguing about it all day. His father had acted nervous. "Your mother's cooking up something really good," he kept saying in the yard. He'd say, "Gosh, it's good to see you, Bud," laughing awkwardly. He had given Randy a *Sports Illustrated* that he must have picked up at the grocery store. "Thought you might like some reading matter, Buddy." Randy seldom read *Sports Illustrated,* though his father had been buying it for years. His father had wanted him to play pro ball after college but that all ended when Randy was hurt. When he quit playing. Quit everything. And everything changed.

And that was when they started calling him "Buddy," or, worse, "Bud." He'd been hearing it all day, from all of them. Though he didn't particularly like his name, Randall Gregory Randall, he could see no "Bud" anywhere among the three words. He had no idea why they did it and he inwardly loathed it. Perhaps it was the tone in their voices, a tone for widows or widowers. He remembered the voices of his relatives when they spoke of his Aunt Rebecca after Uncle Eugene died; and that's when they started calling her again by her childhood nickname Plum.

His mother said outside the bedroom door, "They'll all want stuffing and gravy . . ." but the voices waxed soft again.

No, thought Randy, *I won't*. That's why he had made Teddy stop at the Jack-in-the-Box on the way home from the hospital. The familiar holiday taste of turkey on top of everything else would be too much today. He wanted something simple, tasteless. And dinner was going to be late. He was glad he'd had something to eat, to calm him. He remembered the ride home. The memory was funny to him: something about the way Teddy had acted in the car.

"I'd like a hamburger," Randy had said when Teddy stopped at the intersection. They had said little to each other since leaving the hospital and now the sound of his voice filled the car. They turned their heads as if hearing a sonic boom.

"You hungry?" said Teddy in his big-brother voice.

"I'm sure your mother has dinner ready," said Mary. She was carrying a green-bean casserole to be heated up for the meal.

"Can't you wait?" Teddy said.

Randy shook his head. "I want to go in there."

They looked at each other as if what he had said required them to make a difficult decision.

Mary said, "You'll spoil your dinner, Randy."

"Maybe he just wants a hamburger," said Teddy. Then to Randy, "Is that it, Bud?" And then back to Mary, "They probably don't get hamburgers in that place." Then to Randy, "Is that it?"

Randy, smiling, shook his head no.

"He's just hungry," Teddy said. "A little burger won't hurt anything. Sort of an appetizer."

"Fine," said Mary.

Teddy drove to the outside menu board. Randy leaned out the car window. He said, "I want three hamburgers, cut the onions, and a large order of French fries."

"Wait a minute," said Teddy. "I thought you just wanted a quick burger."

". . . . and a large vanilla shake," Randy said to the speaker. Then to Teddy and Mary, "I've got money."

The voice in the speaker said, "How about an apple turnover with that?"

"No, no," Teddy said firmly and drove up to the window.

Randy ate one burger, the fries and the shake in the car; two burgers waited in a bag in the pocket of his warm-up jacket.

His parents were still in the hall, still whispering.

"Why don't you take that stupid flower out of your hair. You look like a floozie. Nobody wears a geranium in their hair."

He heard his father's footsteps. Then there was silence and then his mother left too. His parents had never understood how far and through what hard surfaces their voices would carry in the house. He had listened to their secrets all his life.

He lay on the bed watching the bedspread flutter above him. He saw some scratches on one of the slats under the mattress of the top bunk. He looked closely and remembered that he had made the scratches years ago with his Scout knife. They formed a rough star, five points. He remembered another scar in wood. It was on a cabinet door in the kitchen. He had seen the scar earlier but had not thought about it until now. There was a disturbing design to the scratches, something Oriental, and they had been glowering down at all of them for months. He imagined his mother touching the door each morning, thinking, We should have this refinished.

He allowed the memory to gel in his mind.

Early morning and everyone is up, getting ready for the day. He and Janet are still living at home, and they have overheard their parents arguing. He heard them as he went to the bathroom to shower, and he hears them now as he goes into the kitchen for breakfast. He pours himself a bowl of cereal and joins Janet at the dining room table. They are silent, exchanging silent glances. He hears his parents in the kitchen; one of them leaves and then comes back, and more words are exchanged: "It's none of your business," his father whispers and his mother says, "It's plenty of my business, half that money is mine and I don't want to lose it. . . . ." Randy goes into the kitchen, puts his bowl in the sink and starts to leave by the back door. But he stops. He sees his father throw something at his mother. She doesn't move, but it misses her head and slams into the cabinet door. It shatters when it hits the floor, and he sees the thick handle of a coffee mug. Anger wells up inside him so quickly that he doesn't know what it is. He grips his father's arm and spins him around. He pushes his father's arm back over his pinstriped shoulder until he thinks the arm may break. His father falls hard to the floor, and then Randy is on top of him with his arm cocked, ready to punch. But something is pulling on him, on his shoulders, and he realizes that it's his mother. His arm comes down out of her grip and his fist grazes his father's head before pounding against the floor.

"Don't, Randy," his mother screams. "Don't, Daddy."

He hears Janet crying behind him and his knuckles ache and then he feels a thud against his face. Everything spins around and he is lying on the floor on his back. He is groggy and feels sick at his stomach. His father is leaning over him, his face blanched. Everything is blurry.

"Are you hurt?"

"Daddy, don't, don't."

"Stop it, stop it."

"Are you hurt?"

"Get away from him."

"Daddy, don't."

The voices collide and mingle and he is pushing with his heels away from his father's blurry face. He pushes until his head strikes something solid. It's the door and he pulls himself up and tries to push his father but his father's great bulk is firm. He pushes again, and his father acts as if all life has gone out of him and he stumbles backward. His mother is now between them saying, "Don't, don't," and his father's face is deep and angry and frightened and he hears himself say: "If you ever do that again I'll get a gun and shoot you." He finds the doorknob and leaves the house and doesn't come home for two days. He stays with a friend who lives in a dormitory at school.

That was his freshman year, his only year, at Rice. He had been accepted on a scholarship but never played baseball. He never played because he had been hurt his senior year, cleated in the ankle as he covered first from the mound on a grounder in the team's next-to-last game. But he had gone to class, failed three of his five freshman courses, and he fell in love with Jean.

If you ever do that again I'll get a gun and shoot you.

They never spoke of that day, never wanting to remember those contorted faces, the fierce unnatural voices, those tiny flesh wounds. They went on living the way they had always lived with each other, in a kind of self-contained rage. But the rooms of the house grew smaller each day. Often he would wake in the morning to find that he had left his window open and his radio on all night, the simple cool wind and the smug distant music wafting in from the world outside. He would stand at his window, looking out at the aged wisteria bush his parents had planted when they bought the house, wanting something.

He saw Jean regularly. She would take him out into the world in her car and later his parents, wringing their hands, would ask who she was and he would say just a girl and then go to his room. When summer came they went to drive-in theaters at night, and they took her son, Jason, on picnics to the country. They spoke of themselves to each other but never of the future, of a future beyond the longing to be somewhere else. Then they got away, she from the father of the child who wanted to marry her and take her to Alaska where he could get work, Randy from his family and the feeling that he had disappointed them all in his failures, in wanting something but not knowing what it was, in not knowing how to proceed with his life. He had had to say "I don't know" far too many times when one of them asked "What are you going to do with yourself?" So he and Jean went to the farm near Brenham that belonged to her aunt and did odd jobs to pay their rent. They stayed three months. Toward the end she cried at night and wouldn't tell him why. Until one morning it came out: "This is not working, I don't love you. I thought I would grow to love you but I don't. I don't love anybody but this little one."

They had been awake all night, separated only by the thin door between the cramped wood-paneled bedroom and the cramped one-window living room. He had heard her crying off and on and murmuring quietly to the baby who lay beside her in the bed.

He said, "I know, I've known for a while."

"Then why have you stayed?"

He said nothing for a long time and then started laughing.

"Don't," she said, and her white-blonde hair shook with emphasis. Her blue eyes flashed and cursed him.

But he laughed; he couldn't stop, though once he muttered through the laughter, "We're a fine pair, aren't we?" "Don't," she screamed and the baby cried.

He laughed. He muttered, "You trying to run away from it all the time and me trying to run to it all the time." He laughed.

"Stop it." She snatched up the baby, hushed him with whispers and caresses. "Don't! You're scaring him."

He attempted apologies, but all he could do was laugh.

She said, "Quit it" and then locked herself in the bedroom.

That was the last time he saw her. He hitched a ride with an old man in an old truck loaded with crates of tomatoes. The old man took him to a vegetable stand in the city near the port where he got a job. Then there was the hospital, the psych ward, the place of the disappointed, the place where they house those who don't know what they want. It was almost two weeks before his therapist would venture a diagnosis: Major Depressive Illness.

The furnace wheezed, and he knew that meant it was cycling off. He didn't want to think about anything else so he allowed his mind to fall slowly into the abyss of sleep. He did not dream but once in his drowsiness he heard a voice say, "Don't!"

The knock on the door was light, a woman's hand, and in came Janet followed by the robust smells of cooking food.

"Dinner's ready," she said. "Mama wanted me to get you up."

He nodded. They smiled at each other, he a little groggy, she cheerful and friendly.

"How you feeling?" He nodded again.

"Everybody's sure been worried about you."

She had left Houston for college in Austin that fall—now home for the holiday. He was certain that she had received reports from his mother, but he was equally certain that she knew little of what had happened. His mother had surely told her not to talk about it but he feared she would try to anyway, as his mother had, and that she'd be hurt when he had nothing to say.

Janet closed the bedroom door and then sat on the bed. A glint of conspiracy enlivened her eyes.

"I want to tell you something," she said. "I can't tell them yet but I wanted to tell you. I'm going to quit school."

The look on her face made him think he was supposed to gasp in surprise. They were silent for several moments.

He said, "Why?"

"I'm going to play the drums in a band, a jazz band." She smiled below her orange hair. "I've played a few gigs with them. They say I've got talent. I've given up the violin for good."

He nodded to show that he agreed; she did have talent. Their parents didn't know it but Janet had been training herself on the drums for years. She used to practice in the garage of Jimmy Madison's parents' house on Jimmy's old drum set. Randy had gone to listen several times and he knew what she wanted.

"They want me to move to Kansas City with them. That's where Corey's from. He's sort of the leader of the band. I think I'm going to go." She smiled to herself. "What do you think?"

He nodded and shrugged his shoulders. She was going; she had packed her bags. He would miss her but there was nothing he could do about it. Her eyes beseeched him to say something.

"Guess what else," she said. "Teddy just told me while Daddy was in the store getting the film." Her voice dropped. "Mary's pregnant." Her eyebrows lifted, dropped. "I think they're going to wait to tell Mom and Dad until things calm down." She thought a moment. "I think it's exciting, a new generation. Don't you?"

He nodded. So many secrets. He thought of the dictionary he kept next to his hospital cot. He said, "An unborn or recently born person, a young person between the periods of infancy and youth, a male or female offspring, son, daughter, one strongly influenced by another or by a place or state of affairs."

Her oval face puckered around her dark eyes, under the orange, greasy-looking bangs, above her pointed chin. "Huh?"

He shook his head.

"Well, I hope it's a girl."

He nodded.

"Teddy's making enough now that they'll do fine. Can you imagine Mary pregnant? She'll blow up like a balloon." Janet sat still, considering. "And what about Teddy. Marriage sure agrees with him. He's really put on weight." She glanced around, said in a confidential voice: "But what about those clothes." They both smiled. "I've never seen him in cowboy boots before."

Neither had Randy. Teddy wore business suits to work but today he had on a western shirt and jeans and black boots.

Randy said, "A new image maybe."

"Yeah." She laughed once. "Oh! And guess what else."

He waited.

"God, there's a lot going on."

He waited.

"I think Mama's living in my room." Again she raised her eyebrows but he said nothing. "All her clothes are in my closet and her shoes too. And I think she started smoking. I found a pack of Kools in the pocket of a dress. Isn't that funny?"

Randy remembered the smell of his mother's breath. He smiled and shook his shoulders to make her think he was laughing.

"She must hide them in there from Daddy."

Randy mumbled, "Something kept from the knowledge of others, a mystery, concealment."

She almost said something but then got up from the bed.

"Can you believe it, I'm going to be an aunt." She looked at him.

"And you're going to be an uncle." Then she said, wistfully, remotely, "A baby," and briefly cupped her stomach with both hands. She walked through the small room, touching things as she talked. "Now all we've got to do is get you well and everything will be settled." She touched an old baseball cap on the dresser top and his high school diploma in its frame and then reached up and touched the last remaining model airplane hanging by a string from the ceiling. It was a P-38 from World War II. The plane turned slowly after she went on, circling the room.

He watched her. Her turquoise sweater and tight black jeans revealed a shapeliness, a woman's breasts and hips, that he had not noticed before. Several bracelets jangled on her arm. A long chain of gold gathered in a knot between her breasts like a loosely knotted tie then dangled across her belly. The chain flapped against the crotch of her pants when she moved. She said, "What's it like in the hospital?" and glanced at him.

"No good," he said.

She stopped at his closet, opened the door, looked in. "You haven't had shock treatment or anything have you?"

He kept quiet, still; she wasn't looking, didn't expect an answer. She took out a robe on its hanger, blue corduroy, a Christmas present from five or six years ago. Holding it before her, pressing its middle to her abdomen with a hand, she looked at herself in the mirror. "I didn't know you still had this. I think I wore it as much as you did." She hung up the robe, touched some other clothes. "How long you gonna be in there?" Her voice was muffled in the closet. She stepped out.

He shrugged, tilted his head. Then he thought of something. He said, "Till all the cows come home, mooing and swinging their tails." His mother had always said that.

Janet smiled. "Oh it won't be that long." She touched the old radio on his nightstand then leaned her head on her arms against the upper bunk. The long gold chain swung out from her body like a rope over a swimming hole and lightly tapped her belly. She looked down at him. Her eyes were so young, so deep, so wondrous with questions. She said, "What happened, Randy, can you tell me? I won't say anything."

A dozen images pulsed through his mind. He saw the events of the past few months flip by like pictures in a viewfinder. He saw bits of his childhood and imagined bits of the future. Janet's face, so full of secrets and probing encouragement, hung above him. The furnace in the attic rumbled and wheezed and came on again. The breeze fluttered the bedspread next to her face. Suddenly he realized what she had been doing: telling him her secrets so that he would tell her his. A sense of betrayal twitched the corners of his mouth.

He said, "I . . . I don't know."

They stared at each other until the voice of their mother pierced the bedroom door: "Let's go, you two, it's on the table."

Randy sat up on the bed.

"Maybe we can talk later," she said.

He nodded. He waited, looking at her.

"Don't tell anybody about what I said," she whispered.

He shook his head. She stared at him a long time and then smiled, the corner of her mouth rising once, twice, as if trying to think of what to say. He thought she wanted to say: I know what you're doing and it's okay: I, at least, understand. That's what that look had always said to him before, when they were young, growing up so close together. If she knew, he wanted her to say it; he tried to encourage her with his eyes. He longed to know what she thought he was doing. Instead, she stepped away.

"Come on, let's eat," she said. "I'm starved."

3. Landscape With Lightning

Randy peered through the window into the oven. His hamburgers were almost ready. He could hear the others in the dining room making talk about how "lovely" the turkey looked and smelled and what a "marvelous" Thanksgiving table his mother had spread.

"Where's Randy?" his father said.

"He's up to something in the kitchen," said his mother. "Randy, come on."

With a spatula he lifted the hamburgers onto a plate and then joined his family in the dining room.

"What is this?" his mother said when he took his seat next to Janet. All the faces were staring at his plate.

"Don't you want any bird?" said his father.

Randy shook his head no, and the others looked around, embarrassed. His father stared at him. He said, "Your mother's been cooking all afternoon for you," and his voice opened a vacancy in the air above the table. Randy sat rigid as he always had when his father challenged him or raised his voice."

Leave him alone," said his mother.

Mary asked, "Shall we pray?" and everyone exchanged glances.

"Certainly we'll pray, if you'd like," said his father. "Would you do us the honor, young lady?"

Randy looked at the parts in everyone's hair as the others bowed their heads. His father's part was low on the left side of his head. Teddy's was higher on the left. Mary's cut squarely down the middle and his mother's was on the right. He couldn't see a part in Janet's hair. He thought for a moment and recalled that when he parted his hair he parted it on the right.

Mary's voice droned, and Randy tried to imagine the baby in her womb, curled behind the pale lavender material of its mother's blouse. But all he got was the image of a fetus floating in a bottle like the one he'd seen at a science fair. The blouse, with buttons to the neck, hung below her waist, he remembered, outside her baggy slacks, and he wondered if she was making believe they were maternity clothes. And Teddy, with his new image: maybe he wants a boy, a boy who will grow up to be a ranch hand, "a kicker"—that's what they were called in high school.

Mary said, "Bless all of us assembled here today. Amen."

They all looked up, pleased with themselves, and started passing platters of food, talking among themselves. Randy passed everything except Mary's green beans, of which he took a heaping portion. The mushroom sauce soaked his hamburger buns.

Then Teddy stood up. He had a camera in his hand. "I want to get you all together," he said, backing into the living room. "Lean in," he said. "Lean in over the table so you're all in the picture." His mother had to turn in her seat. Janet leaned forward and draped an arm over Randy's shoulder. Their faces were almost touching when Teddy said, "Say whiskey," and, smiling himself as an example, clicked the picture. "Let me get one more," Teddy said but he was called down by a chorus of "No."

"Mother," said Janet, reaching for a roll. "I like the flower. It's pretty. It makes you look festive."

"Oh," said his mother. "Thank you, dear." She reached up and almost touched the geranium but then brought her hand down on Randy's wrist, giving it a squeeze. She looked at him, smiling, and then, her gaze spanning the table as if to speak only to his father, she said: "Randy gave it to me." The others said, "Ah."

Randy, his face flushed, stared at the food on his plate. He was afraid to look up, afraid to see them looking at him with their inquiring smiles, afraid Janet's face would be grinning at him and make him return an expression that would tell the others the two of them were sharing secrets. He could feel Janet's eyes lingering on him. He thought, Please don't make me look at you.

His father said flatly, "Who wants yams?"

When the bowl came to Randy he passed it to Janet and in that instant of contact, as each held the bowl, he felt something drawing his eyes up to her. He saw again the secrets in her eyes, a glint of light, the slightly lowered lids, that mysterious penetrating bond that had linked them all through childhood in a way that nothing else in the world is linked. It had no definition, nothing specific. It said simply, I know what you're doing.

He felt her eyes leave him when she took the bowl. She said, oddly, as she spooned a yam onto her plate, "Thank you, Randy."

He was embarrassed by the long moment that had passed between them and sensed a lull in the talk among the others as if each had stopped to watch them or to listen for anything else that might be said. But soon the business of dinner resumed.

"Is butter on the table?"

"We only have margarine."

"Pass the spuds, please."

"Who still needs turkey?"

"I do."

"Your beans are delicious."

"Don't I get a napkin?"

"Look at this."

"What?"

"There's something gross on this fork."

"Well get another one."

"We should have wine."

"We can't, dear, it gives Daddy a headache."

"Pepper. Where's the pepper?"

"It's right next to you."

"What'd you do to this meat, Mother?"

"It's barbecued. . . ."

"It's smoked."

"It's very tasty."

"Very juicy."

"Yes . . . well . . . save room for dessert."

He submerged himself beneath the talk until it was nothing but amorphous noise, ripples above the surface of his thoughts. He wanted to return to something that had flitted through his mind earlier. It had come to him while Janet was in his closet and again when he passed her the yams. He summoned the face of Janet and then remembered being in his closet one night, sitting amid shoes in the darkness, smelling the sour dusty odor of his clothes, afraid of something in his room. What? He'd been there a long time when the door opened; it was Janet in a nightgown. She said only: "It's gone, Randy."

Now he knew the secret they were sharing, knew what Janet thought: you're hiding in your closet and you won't come out until whatever is in the dark room has gone away. He wanted her to say, "It's gone, Randy," but he knew it wouldn't work this time. It was too simple to work again, and she had changed.

Something in his chest stirred, a tentative pain, and he was thankful when he heard his name mentioned. "You want potatoes?" It was Janet again, holding the bowl out for him. He thought she might be trying to get his attention. He shook his head no.

He slipped back under the surface and for several minutes he heard only the clinking of silverware against china and an occasional "Mmmm, delicious." Randy ate his hamburgers quickly and then the beans and he sipped his iced tea. He waited for the others to finish. But a conversation had sprung up at the table.

"Remember that trip to Garner," said Teddy. "The one when we rode horses. These two were just grunts." He nodded toward Janet and Randy.

"Oh yeah," said his father slowly.

"And Randy got lost," said Janet.

"That's the one," said Teddy.

"I remember," said his father. "We looked all afternoon in a rainstorm for him, riding those stupid horses."

"What happened?" said Mary.

His mother laughed: "Oh, we found him finally."

"But we found the horse first, remember," said Teddy. "God, we thought the horse had thrown him and killed him or something."

"Where was he?" said Janet. "I can't remember."

"Remember, the little jerk was sitting under a tree on a hill and when we rode up he yelled out, 'Where you been? I thought you were lost.' He was on the verge of tears."

They all laughed and Randy felt the warmth of a blush spread up his neck and over his face.

"That's right," said Janet, loudly over the laughter. "And Daddy almost shook the life out of him."

The laughter turned to awkward coughs and everyone seemed to be trying to look away, out a window or something, until finally it was only the clinking of forks and knives again.

"I don't remember shaking Randy," his father said, glancing between Teddy and Janet. Everyone was quiet, faces turned slightly down. Their eyes darted like the eyes of cheaters.

"Why don't we just drop it," said his mother.

"I remember it," Janet said, and all eyes stopped on her.

"What's it matter," said his mother. "It was so long ago."

"I remember it clearly," said Teddy. He paused as if wondering whether to go on. "First, you kind of hugged him and then, I guess, when you realized he was all right, you said, 'Don't ever do that again,' and then you grabbed him by the shoulders and shook him like an old rug. I remember it because that stupid hat he always wore, the Robin Hood hat with the feather, remember, it fell in the mud and we had to clean it up in the river later."

"I never did that. I don't remember any of that."

"Yeah, you did," said Teddy. "He cried like a little baby."

"I remember it," said Janet, "because Randy wouldn't come out of the tent all the next day. He kept saying, 'I hope lightning strikes Daddy.'" She laughed.

His father said, "Well, now I sort of remember the lightning stuff but I don't remember any of that other business."

Randy did. He remembered feeling frightened at being alone under the tree in the rain and at having let his horse wander away. He had been searching for them among the hills, thinking he'd find them at any turn but every turn had seemed the same. He had remembered being told that the best thing to do was to remain in one place and allow rescuers to find you. So he got down from the horse and climbed onto some rocks that formed the base of a hill and he went up the hill until he found the tree and sat down underneath it to wait. The tree creaked and strained in the wind, making eerie moaning sounds, and drops of rain plopped onto his hat. It was the first time he had ever thought that he might die, that he would die someday like his grandmothers and grandfathers, that he would disappear like Carmen, the dog his father had brought home one day when Randy was small, very small, saying,

The oddest thing happened, an old man, "a bum really," crossing a

street at a stoplight downtown had paused in front of his car, looked at him hard through the windshield and opened his overcoat to reveal a puppy clutching to the crook of his arm; "and then he came to my window—I don't know why he picked me—he came to the window, the light was about to change, and he held up the puppy like it was a prize." And the man said, "Mister, I can't care for it, you take it, her name's Carmen." His father said, No he couldn't. "But that old bum grinned like a fifty-dollar bill and he said, 'Sure you can,' and then he threw the dog in the window. When I looked up the old guy had crossed the street and was running away and just then the light changed."

His father had told the story with sparkling eyes, looking down at the dog shivering on the porch. Teasing, his father had said, "That's how we got Randy, isn't it, Mother?" And they all laughed. Carmen disappeared the week of his seventh birthday. "She's gone to heaven, sweetheart," his mother said. Sitting in the rain and the chill that afternoon he had tried to prepare himself for heaven and what he would say to God. But he didn't know how, what was expected of him, and he was very thankful when his family appeared beyond the rocks at the base of the hill with his horse in tow. He remembered feeling like a survivor, someone who should have been carried on shoulders and cheered. Instead, his father yelled at him and shook him and knocked his cap off. And all the way to the campsite he had imagined his father alone under a tree in the rain and the lightning.

The others at the table were still talking about it.

"Please, that's enough," said his mother.

"Randy, is any of this true?" said his father.

Just then Randy stood and left the table.

The catcher's mitt was still on the bench where he'd left it so he laid himself down and put the mitt under his head. For a moment he imagined the others still at the dinner table, excited, hissing at each other about who was at fault, who had driven him away. The image soon receded and was replaced by another.

The five of them in the old station wagon. His father and mother in front, the three children in back with Randy, wearing a baseball uniform, in the middle.

Where had they been? Practice? A game? He tried to recall it, but for an instant his mind wandered out of the scene to the day around him. The shadows of the trees and the garage were long and sullen, clinging hard to the ground. Then he remembered his father saying, "It wasn't your fault. You had your stuff. No back-up from the infield," and he was thrown back into the scene.

It's a familiar street in the neighborhood, lined with shopping centers and restaurants. Signs pass by. Lights. "I want Chuck Wagon," says Janet. "We always go to Chuck Wagon." Teddy says, "I'm sick of Chuck Wagon. How about Dairy Queen?" It goes on and on. His mother enters the argument, suggesting they eat at Whataburger, and then his father sides with Janet. They go on and on, arguing as if it's a family rule, as if nothing can be done without first arguing and kicking and crying. Janet and Teddy lean across him and jab at each other. His mother screams, "Stop that," and turns in her seat to smack Janet's knee. Janet says, "You never hit Randy." Teddy is laughing, taunting her. His father, glancing into the rearview mirror, threatens to stop the car and make all of them get out. "You never hit Randy," Janet wails. They go on and on. At last Randy slams his glove against the ceiling of the car, two, three, four times. "Shut up!" His father scrutinizes him in the mirror and his mother looks over her shoulder. Her face is stunned as if she's been slapped. He says, "You're all stupid." There is a long silence until his father turns the car into the parking lot of Chuck Wagon.

The face of his father came into focus. He was standing over the bench, looking down at Randy. He said, "Hey, Bud, you okay?"

The opening to the cavity suddenly quivered and he said, "Why did you shake me?" The words sounded distant, hoarse, as if someone else had said them.

His father's eyes went tight, and he let out a noisy breath. His mouth had the downward curve of a penitent facing the minister. He looked away at the yard. He shivered and drove his hands deep into his pockets. He said, "It's better to remember the good times, Buddy. Why can't you remember them?"

Slowly his father's face changed. It became firm, driving downward somehow as if he were getting angry, as if he wanted to say, Snap out of it, get a grip on yourself. The face said, I've made my life and I'm living with it, now you make yours.

Troubled, uncertain, his father glanced up at the sky and then looked down at Randy on the bench. His face had mellowed again, and when their eyes met a thread of anticipation snaked its way out of Randy's heart to his mind. Yes go on, he thought.

"It's gonna be chilly tonight," he said, turning away. "Maybe we'll have a fire. You always liked fires."

The back door opened. Randy heard the screen clang and then Teddy was standing beside his father in the thinning light of the beautiful day. They said nothing for a good while, taking in the afternoon, then Teddy asked, "Say, you want to throw some?"

"Sure," said his father. "Sure. Come on." "How about you, Bud?" Teddy said but Randy didn't answer. He pulled the mitt from behind his head and handed it to his father.

"Hey, Randy." It was Teddy, calling to him from the yard where he and his father had been playing pitch for half an hour or so. "Why don't you toss a few before it gets dark."

"Yeah, come on," said his father.

He stood up and watched them for a moment. Teddy's awkward way of throwing the ball had always amused Randy. Teddy had always tried hard but he never had been able to master it with any kind of rhythm. Teddy threw one wide and his father had to leap out from his squatting position to catch it. He threw a couple more, one into the grass and the other high.

"Here," said Teddy, tossing the ball to Randy. "I'll ump."

Randy placed his foot where Teddy's boot had been in the grass and he threw an easy one to his father, who was now standing behind the make-believe plate near the wall of the garage.

"That's it," his father said. "Warm up first."

With each throw Randy felt stronger, looser, until he was starting to hurl the ball. After each pitch his father would shake his mitted hand as if the pitch had been a zinger. He squatted behind the plate again.

"Come on, now, burn it in here," he said, smacking the pocket of the mitt. "Come on, Babe."

Randy sensed Teddy just behind him, leaning forward to judge the pitches. Teddy would say softly, "Ball," or, "That one's in there." Now Teddy said, "Okay, you've got a man at the plate. Let's see what you can do."

His father was giving him signals, his hand at his crotch. One finger for a fast ball, two for a curve, three for the reliable sinker Randy had been known for in his glory days. He made four pitches and Teddy called them two balls, two strikes. His father signaled for a fast ball. Randy wound up and heaved it as hard as he could, following-through perfectly, bringing his right foot to the ground at the instant the ball met the mitt.

Teddy said, "Nope, nope, that's a ball. Okay, three and two, let's see you get this guy."

Randy strained to see his father's hand in the dusk light. Three fingers, the sinker. The mitt went down almost to the grass as a target. His father crouched lower, preparing to trap the ball, and Randy saw him wince with the effort. Randy gripped the ball along its seams, calling up the oft-practiced motion and the required flip of the wrist that used to send pulses of excitement through his body when he did it right. The charge of anticipation now pulsed through him, up his back, into his hair. He brought his hands up, looked closely at the mitt, went into his motion, kicked his leg, carefully lolling his weight backward and then upward and then over and then forward, and he let the ball fly with an audible "oomph." But as soon as he released it he knew he had done it too soon. He knew it would be high. He saw the ball rising as his airborne foot sought its landing place. And his father's face, a mask of surprise, lurched as he tried to move away from the pitch. The mitt came up but not in time. The ball grazed the leather and zipped just past his father's ear, then smacked the wall of the garage. His father fell backward and landed hard on the ground.

"Jesus, Randy," Teddy hissed. "What'd you do that for?"

"Hey, boy," cried his father, who couldn't have heard Teddy. He seemed to laugh. "Wow. That one almost got me."

"It slipped," Randy said to Teddy. He saw an ugly and pointed kind of fear in his brother's face.

Teddy said, "You could have hurt him, you little jerk," and then he brushed past Randy to go to his father. Randy watched Teddy help his father up, two figures in the gray light now. They were brushing off his clothes. Then they were still. The three of them looked at each other for a long moment, and Randy almost said it again: "It slipped." But what good would it do? Teddy wouldn't believe it and his father would say, "Kind of rusty, eh?"

Randy hurried toward the house, but the house seemed suddenly far away and he to be walking in place. He forced himself onward and his mind searched wildly for something, as if flipping through index cards, until, as he crossed the patio, it came to a series of words: A male parent, the first person of the Trinity, one deserving respect and love. . . . And here was the door.

He wanted to get away. He wanted to be gone from them. But the screen wouldn't open; the latch was stuck. It had been sticking off and on for years. He glanced back. He yelled, "Why don't you fix this thing!"

He kicked the screen and kicked it again until the latch popped free and he opened the door.

4. Here We Are in Moonlight

When he entered the kitchen the faces of the three women jerked toward him. He walked past them and went through the house to the phone in the hall. He called directory assistance.

"Which city?"

"Houston."

"Go ahead."

"Yellow Cab Company, please."

Janet was standing next to him, holding a dish towel. He knew she must have heard what he'd said into the phone.

"What are you doing?"

He didn't look at her and didn't answer. When the recording had given him the number he quickly made the call.

"Don't leave, Randy," she said. "It's stupid to leave now."

The woman on the phone said it would be fifteen minutes. He put the receiver in its cradle and stared at it. He didn't want to look at Janet. He tried to leave but she stepped in front of him. She said, "Don't you think this has gone on long enough?" He had to look at her now and when he did he saw that something had changed in her eyes. The secret was missing.

"Let it go, Randy," she said.

He squeezed past her and went to the living room. Janet followed him. And here was his mother, holding a dishtowel and a plate in her hands. She stepped toward him. "What's wrong, darling?" He paused and looked at her but then walked on.

Janet said, "He's leaving."

"No," said his mother.

He got his jacket and opened the door. His mother called to him, but he went outside and down the sidewalk to the curb. He could imagine the scene inside the house. Teddy and his father would have come in by now and would have explained what had happened. The four would be standing in the living room, embarrassed that Mary had seen all of this and saying with their eyes, What should we do? What have we done to deserve this?

Randy zipped up his jacket and sat on the curb between Teddy's Volvo and Janet's Toyota. It was a clear night. A wisp of orange remained in the western sky. Stars were beginning to shine and a full moon hung low over the houses to the east. Surrounding the moon were several rings of stark white mist as if it were the center of a great target. The outlines of the houses and the trees in their yards were distinct in the moonlight.

Yes. His father was right. It would be a perfect night for a fire. A perfect night for them to take their seats in a comfortable room or to stand before the hearth warming their hands and hearts with cheerful talk and strong hot drinks. A perfect night to bring out the photo albums and to remember.

The door to the house opened then closed and footsteps clapped against the sidewalk coming up behind him. It was at least two people and when the footsteps stopped he heard his mother say, "What a gorgeous night."

His father said, "Hey, Bud, ole Teddy's starting a fire. Why don't you come back in. You've still got some time, he says."

I can't, he thought, and he shook his head no.

His mother stepped around him into the street between the cars. In her hands was a wad of aluminum foil. She knelt and looked into his face. The sadness in her eyes was gone now; she had the look of someone who had accepted a certain fact in her life and wanted to go on.

"I brought you some pie," she said. "It's pecan. A frozen one, I'm afraid, but it still tastes pretty good." She handed him the wad of foil. It was warm in his hands. "We'll just wait here with you," she said, smiling. "You cold?"

He shrugged and shook his head no.

"Oh my gosh," his father said. "The magazine."

Randy heard him walking away up the sidewalk. "Don't let him leave until I get back," he said, and then the door opened and closed. He and his mother looked at each other. It was apparent she wanted to say something to sooth him but couldn't think of anything. She sat on the curb next to him.

"Look at all the stars," she said. "You don't see them like this too often in the city."

They were silent, gazing into the sky.

She said, "Rings around the moon, eat it with a spoon." She must have seen something in his eyes. "We used to say that when I was a girl. I never did know what it meant." A noise, almost a laugh, slipped out of her nose. "I remember I'd lie in the yard for hours trying to figure out what made those rings. It was always kind of scary, but it fascinated me." She gave a little grunt of wonder and turned to Randy. "Do you know?"

The question unsettled him. He couldn't recall his mother ever asking him such a question, a question that required a rational, reasoned answer, an answer that would come from knowledge rather than emotion.

He said, "No."

A car turned at the corner and then the yellow splash of light from its high beams illuminated the magnolia in the yard across the street. The car crept up to them and stopped. A man's voice said, "You call a cab?" and Randy stood up.

"Oh, wait here he comes," said his mother.

His father was breathing hard when he got up to them. He handed Randy the magazine through the open cab door. His mother leaned in and kissed him on the lips.

"So long, Bud," said his father. "Don't take any guff off those doctors now." Randy could see him smiling over his mother's shoulder. "Be good, dear," she said and then stepped back. He thought his father was going to come up and shake his hand or hug him, but he didn't, so Randy closed the door.

"Memorial Hospital, downtown," he told the driver.

He gazed at his parents through the window; they had the appearance of a young couple posing for a photograph. His father's arm was around his mother's waist, and they stood perfectly still in the middle of the street, smiling in a way that pulled on him, made him want to get out of the car. They waved.

Behind them was the moon with its rings, and the light from the moon caressed everything and everything was calm and simple in the light. The car lunged forward and he looked back, pressing his face against the door window. Their figures, hazy and blue-tinted, blended gradually until they became one figure, receding. He turned in the seat to look out the rear window; they were a distant shadow now in the moonlight. He waved but he knew they couldn't see him, and he sensed something final in the gesture as if perhaps it was the last time he would ever wave to them. The car turned a corner and their dark outline disappeared.

He twisted around in his seat and as he did so he bumped his head on the ceiling of the car. That's when he realized he'd forgotten his cap. He started to tell the driver to stop, to turn around. But no, it would be embarrassing to go back. They would think he had returned because of them. How would he explain? The thought of it somehow made his leaving complete, more so than the waving hands, the hugs, the kisses. It now was an act of necessity, a fact. He settled himself for the drive and after a moment looked out the door window at the sky. It was a perfect night. There were thousands, millions, of stars, the final products of a beautiful day. They stretched far away, as far as he could see. He remembered a teacher saying once that there were more stars than people, that the universe was so vast all the stars would never be counted. New stars forming, old ones dying.

This sent his mind exploring until, rising up, up above everything, soaring up, he had a view of the earth as if from heaven. There was Africa, there Europe, here America. He could see stars hanging over everything, over all the oceans and all the cities and all the houses in the world, and over all the people in the houses and over all the hearts inside the people. He imagined a star for every person who had ever lived and for every person who would ever be born. Every good person and every bad. He imagined a star for his mother and for his father and one each for Teddy and Janet. And then there was one for himself. He saw it moving among the others—so many others, all the same—and his star collided gently with each one, bounced free, paused to apologize and then moved on. This was his life, he thought. He knew he was alive because he could see the stars, and he knew the stars would be there forever, each moving across the sky in its own slow pace, each shining down on a solitary heart.

A chill tingled across his shoulders, and he turned up the collar of his jacket. They were on Lyman Street now, and the lights of stores and businesses passed by. The collected light along the street, rising up, obscured the stars. He could hear the raspy chatter of the taxi's radio, calling drivers to various addresses in the city. They all were going somewhere or returning to something, someone. He thought of his life, where he was going and to what he was returning, and with a sudden strange quiver in the recesses of his body he saw everything clearly, as if all along he had needed only to look up into a deep perfect night for a perfect vision of the past and the future.

He would check out of the hospital as soon as the doctor would allow it and he would take an apartment. Yes. He'd take an apartment but not here, not in Houston. He'd move to Dallas or Austin. He'd buy furniture for the apartment and maybe a car. His parents would help. He'd work; he could find a job and save his money. And maybe he'd return to school, a few classes at first until he hit stride. There were colleges in Dallas and Austin. And maybe there would be a girl, a woman, someone his age, a student. They would go to movies and eat out and maybe live together. People would know them as Randy and Cheryl. Or Randy and Charlotte. Or Randy and Chris. He liked names that began with C. He thought of Teddy and Mary. Yes. There would be another woman in his future. And other Thanksgivings.

He remembered the pie. He made a small opening in the foil and held it up to his nose. The sweet aroma made something clutch in his throat. The cavity in his chest began to swell as if filling with sea water and the opening at the top of the cavity fluttered and expanded. Suddenly he had a great urge to talk. He wanted to tell someone of his plans for the future. He blinked several times and then leaned forward, across the front seat.

"It's pecan pie," he said to the driver, a young man with a beard and long hair. "It's yours."

The driver glanced at Randy. "Oh thanks," he said. "But I can't take your pie, man. Wasn't that your mom and dad?"

He nodded and felt a smile pushing on his face.

"You keep it, man," said the driver. "Spent the day at my old lady's house before going on duty. She had the works."

Randy almost said something, but the driver answered a call on his radio, muttering into the microphone that he had a fare and would be "in service" for half an hour. Then he began joking with the dispatcher. Sitting back in the seat, Randy thought of the "works" he had passed up that afternoon and realized he was hungry. He put the magazine on his lap as a table and unwrapped the foil. It was a large triangle of pie, and the ripply faces of pecan halves shone up at him. He picked off a pecan and ate it as he watched the lights go by. Then he took a bite of the pie, and when he swallowed it went down easily. Another bite and another and soon he was gulping down huge chunks of pie.

When he had finished he looked at the crumbs on the foil and then molded the foil into a ball. He held the ball in his hand, squeezing it into an aluminum marble, and he felt the strength in his hand as he squeezed it. The marble pricked his palm, a simple pain, a pain that would last only a second. He released his grip and the pain went away. He squeezed it again and felt the pain and then relaxed his hand and the pain went away. It was as easy, as simple, as the throwing of a ball.

He rolled down the window and tossed the aluminum marble out into the night along Lyman Street. It glittered like a star as it arced away from him. In a pocket of his jacket he found a piece of paper—his pass from the hospital. He gripped it between two fingers and sat there, very still in his thoughts, letting the chill wind blow across his face.

Dalrymple's Jackpot

1.

Dalrymple stood stunned, paralyzed, incredulous . . . and up welled the venom. "I been fucked!" he shouted without thinking, and everybody, an old-lady customer included, glanced around bug-eyed and silent, shocked by the vulgarity and its shameful truth.

This on the day there in the store when together with half a dozen other loafers and hotshots, salesmen they were called, he saw a bleak and violent and inconvenient future flashing on the screens of maybe forty color television sets arrayed for easy inspection on the carpeted shelves against the long front wall. Some of them—the older guys in gray suits, fake school ties and black wingtips—couldn't help giving off sniggers and shy sad embarrassed smiles. The younger ones—Ripley for instance in his creamy three-piece with the wide lapels and the bell-bottom pants—just grinned and dragged on their Marlboros and offered up a silent thanks to somebody, the government maybe or the God of Peace, that at least it wasn't them with the awful luck.

"Can you believe it," Dalrymple said. "Eight! Why eight?"

He glanced among their faces and then in a daze of disbelief let himself fall backwards into a cellophane-covered recliner whose new black Naugahyde complained of the outrage.

"Eight."

"Christ . . . eight!"

"That ought to teach him to gamble."

A dash of masculine laughter brought hot blood to his face.

"Eight . . . shit!"

The whispers hovered above him like a threatening thundercloud. That shapely numeral in the elegant Set of Evens, so like the luscious curves of a woman's fine body, had in an instant turned ugly and evil, an old whore waving a butcher's knife. It seemed to be everywhere around him, like an invading enemy of angry eight-shaped whores, a stupendous crowd of murderers descending from a vile and noxious vapor.

"Let's see," said Johnson, the asshole with the mouth, also known as Buttface to a few of the crew. "That's three hundred and sixty-five minus three hundred and fifty-seven, isn't it? All those possibilities." He laughed, low and mean. "But no, sure enough looks like we got us a draf-tee on our hands."

"Shut up," whispered McCleary.

"Saigon-bound too."

"Eight . . . shit!" somebody repeated.

It was his lottery number. He'd be called up for sure; he'd be going over. Like curious buzzards waiting to see if the rabbit on the highway was about to get his from a speeding pickup truck, they had gathered that quiet July morning in 1971. They were at the front of the store where the ceiling lights were kept low and the air, cool and clean because of it, tenderly vibrated with that animated and all-encompassing TV hum. Ripley's number had already been announced: 286. The bastard; it was always that way with him; and Dalrymple cursed the day of his own birth. June 15, 1952, would thereafter and forevermore be a blackened page in the biography of his life. He even, silently, cursed his mother.

The others stood in a stunned kind of silence watching the vast collage of TV screens as the two old cranks from the Defense Department turned the wire cage and then reached in for the next number. But none of them cared anymore; they'd seen what they came to see. Ripley had gotten off and Dalrymple was going over. Poor son. He sat there, his elbows on the arms of the recliner, his hands linked before his mouth, staring into a bleak and violent and inconvenient future, staring at nothing.

"Tough luck," said Johnson, the third youngster in the squad of salesmen, 4F and deferred, a year older anyway and out of it. "I mean really tough luck. I mean add in two aces and another eight and you'd be holding the Dead Man's Hand."

"Shut up," said McCleary, the assistant manager, a good man.

"I didn't mean anything," said Johnson, laughing again.

"Well shut up anyway."

Dalrymple felt their stares, their shaking heads; he felt the pity too and the contempt. The moment lasted like the long aching silence in the woods that follows a shotgun blast.

"What are y'all staring at?" asked a defensive Dalrymple.

"He's right, guys," said Henry McCleary. "The party's over, let's get back to it, we got customers."

"'Gratulations, Rip," somebody said and the others took it up, slapping his shoulder or shaking his hand before dispersing. They filed past Dalrymple, glancing down with rueful or wry faces, patting him on the crossed knee and muttering their apologies. Then they spread out across the showroom floor, weaving through the appliances and the furniture on this side of the center aisle, the displays of lawn mowers, tires and auto batteries on the far side. Only Ripley, a kind of friend, stopped.

"Eight.. . . . shit!" he said, and Dalrymple heard the insincerity in it, the undertones of excitement and relief and phony concern.

"I been fucked, man."

"This is true, old hoss."

"I mean fucked!"

Ripley, a handsome kid with a wife, an early baby and at least two girlfriends, whistled in sympathy between his perfect teeth but couldn't contain a faint wavering smile of victory.

"What are you gonna do, Dal?"

Dalrymple glanced up, but he didn't, he couldn't, answer and soon Ripley left him alone to go call his women, to boast of his own good fortune. Dalrymple sat in the recliner for a long time as the morning passed away. Salesmen and customers walked by, walked around him, but he was only vaguely aware of them. *Am I then to die in that war before I can legally drink, or even vote, or even see myself fully grown?* When it was almost lunchtime he got up and left the store without saying a word to anyone.

2.

Dalrymple flushed, zipped and stepped to the rust-stained sink in the reeking men's room to wash his hands and comb his hair. He took his time with it, dawdling, loitering in the pleasant solitude. He'd been worthless all day of course, hadn't done a hundred dollars worth of business (sold two tires to a man who didn't need to be sold), and he was glad the day was coming to an end. He had been plagued by the whispers—*drafted*—and the guarded glances and the pathetic smiles of his co-workers. So he had tried his best to avoid them, taking a long lunch break by himself but without eating and hanging out the rest of the time with Calvin, the chief mechanic, back in the garage.

"Uh-oh, here he come, watch out now," was Calvin's greeting every time Dalrymple wandered out, and those great yellow teeth of his showed kindly behind his heavy black lips.

More often than not they just stood together behind the large battered podium in the corner of the garage where the work orders were kept and tended, smoking and chatting and observing as the other mechanics busted tires or changed the oil in a car resting on a hoist high above them. Sometimes Dalrymple sat on the front-end alignment rack and stared at the littered and greasy floor as Calvin sat quietly beside him or went slowly about his duties. If a customer came in, or another salesman with an order, Calvin handled it and then took his seat again. The loud wrenching noises, the cursing and laughter of the men, their crude voices as they called to each other, the smells of motor oil and auto exhaust and manly labor, of Calvin's sweet cherry pipe tobacco—it all eased the hard knot of injustice that had already formed in Dalrymple's heart. He had worked in this garage for Calvin the summer of his sophomore year, back in those simpler days. Theirs was a friendship that had evolved out of kid-teasing and rough toil and illicit beers (for Dalrymple at least) drunk from cans as he and the four black men, three of whom were different black men then, lounged in the bed of Calvin's '51 Chevy pickup out back of the store on warm summer evenings after work. The teasing never ended, and when Dalrymple became a salesman Calvin started calling him "Mr. Dal."

"What you be hiding from today, Mr. Dal?" Calvin asked at one point, and they shared a certain look full of a certain knowledge, a certain intimacy that slashed through the hypocrisy and the absurdity and got right to the heart of things: Clyde Dalrymple was no salesman and never would be; he was meant for other things—maybe higher, maybe lower—but something else.

"Soldiering ain't so bad," Calvin said after he heard the talk. Dalrymple hadn't mentioned it. "It'll make a man of you sure enough, it did me, and it'll show you a few things."

"Like how to kill?"

"Some of that."

"And how to die?"

Calvin just glanced at him.

"And how to drink whiskey without falling over?"

"Some of that too."

"And how to catch the clap?"

"Oh now, Mr. Dal, you be careful."

They looked at each other. Calvin's eyes, like his teeth, were yellow where the eyeballs showed and watery around the rims and his face was huge and rubbery and very black. His skin was moist and craggy and deeply pocked in the cheeks, giving him the appearance of having lived a hard life. Of the forty-odd employees at Green's, Calvin was the only one that Dalrymple had ever completely trusted. For one thing he could keep a secret and for another he didn't steal, anything, not even your trust.

"You gotta learn to take it easy, Mr. Dal. Things could be worse, they sure could, a lot worse, just imagine."

Dalrymple didn't want to imagine that; he wanted to hide. So he had spent a lot of time in the john too. Every hour or so he'd step in, try a leak, comb his hair, straighten his tie and then stand there gazing at himself in the mirror that was smudged and defiled with greasy fingerprints and a few words of graffiti wisdom. He looked at himself, read the words in the dim light, anything to pass the time until five o'clock. And avoid those smiles.

Not bad, he'd think of his wavy image in the cheap mirror, tolerable at least under the circumstances . . . and he'd give himself the once-over again. Vanity was one of his faults, he knew, but he couldn't help himself; it was a family trait; he got it honest, as his father would say. He liked to look at himself, to see what others saw, to appraise and appreciate and correct if need be. He had broad beefy shoulders and strong thick arms, a result of the bar bells and three years of bull-pen pitching on his high school team, but his chest was still a bit sunken and narrow ,which caused his clothes to hang on him strangely. He was always fidgeting with his jacket, tugging at the lapels, smoothing out the pockets with his large though delicate hands, hands like an Amazon woman's, the fingers long and slender and almost without knuckle, an odd and offending deformity, as he considered it, for a man like Dalrymple. It was because of his weak hands and his size—medium height, about 170 on the scales—that he wasn't and never would have been a great pitcher. Of this fact he was always being reminded by his coaches and his father, and so it was easy for him to give it up when the time came and to go on with a different kind of life. Girls for instance: girl-women.

He was a decent-looking man (enough women thought so) with a long squarish face, marred by a few pimples and a cleft chin. His dark hooded eyes owned the qualities of kindness and thoughtfulness and a certain hard-edged intensity that made him seem older than his nineteen years, as well as a subtle kind of raw and untrained intelligence. At least this is what he liked to think, because he'd been told that by a couple of women, girls really, including his ex-wife, once, long ago now. Angie: still when he thought of her, as he did a few dozen times a day, his chest went tight and his heart thumped threateningly with lust and longing and jealousy and a beautiful hatred. Nineteen, barely out of high school, already married and divorced and with a kid: How had that happened? And how had this happened?

"Because you're a fuck-up," he whispered to the mirror. "Getting Angie pregnant and her barely seventeen and still a Tigerette with her pompons and her tutu and her teeth still in braces. And now this, a kind of pay-back, I guess. You're a fuck-up, that's all, a wiener, a slimeball, you baboon's butt . . . no don't talk like that. Just shut your mouth."

His empty stomach had been giving him trouble all afternoon, a bad case of the silent farts, and as he stood there in the stench of workingman's piss and too-sweet disinfectant, he started to feel light-headed and queasy in his lower regions. Beads of sweat popped out all over his face and his hands trembled as he forced the comb through his short dark hair, already falling out at the crown. So he rinsed his face and washed his hands again with the gray gritty soap they kept for the mechanics and he tried again to make himself right to face the world.

Dalrymple was a snappy dresser in those days. Nothing like Ripley with his pastel suits and his wild high-collared shirts and those crazy ties that looked like dope dreams or images out of a lava lamp, but he did all right with what he had. His taste ran to more subdued colors, dark blues and maroons with occasional flares of red or green.

On his feet he alternated between black tassels and cordovan penny loafers depending on his mood and his color scheme for the day. Like all the salesmen at Green's, he did his shopping at Marco's Men's Store down the block, a rather loud and garish place that stocked lots of polyester, wickedly striped shirts and Sansa-belt slacks. For two years he'd been building up his wardrobe, adding a piece or two every month, a new sport coat whenever he came into a little extra in his commission check. Though it was hard for him (did a green paisley tie go with a gray shirt and a blue sport coat?) he liked looking good, manly and tidy and stylish. It gives you confidence in yourself, he believed, puts you on a sure footing. When a man looks his best he does his best was Dalrymple's belief, which was his father's belief too.

"Let 'em see you coming," his father, a gas company executive, had advised. "But nothing outlandish. Keep it elegant."

"Elegant," Dalrymple said to the mirror. "Yeah, right."

He dried his hands and face with a paper towel and had to pick away the linty damp pieces of paper that stuck to the five o'clock whiskers on his jaw. Then he took a drink of water to help calm his stomach, cupping his hands under the faucet, smelling the bitter rust in the sink and no telling what was down in that dark drain. He checked himself once more and concentrated on his eyes. Were they out of kilter? The left one always seemed lower than the right, mashed in somehow, flattened as if he'd been dropped on his head as a child, another odd deformity. He periodically asked his mother or Angie about this, but after a quick glance they would tell him he was crazy, his eyes were fine. Dalrymple knew better, he could see it, the looking glass didn't lie, and he often tried to straighten things up. He tried it now, the fingers of his right hand pulling down on the brow, the fingers of the left pushing up, blurring his vision in an amusing yet disturbing blast of distortion. Maybe it was the way he pressed his face into his Dutch wife of a pillow at night, and at that moment he vowed to start sleeping on his back, like a man. For a while he just played with his face, pushing and pulling, muttering to himself, "You creep, you retard, you baboon's butt," until his image in the mirror caused him to laugh out loud, a harsh low panting noise that sounded even to Dalrymple like the murmuring of his heart's despair.

3.

Just then he heard his name called over the loudspeaker. Somebody was waiting for him at the main sales counter. He assumed it was a customer and he cursed the intrusion. It meant work; it meant more than likely he'd have to do something.

He stepped out, checking his fly, hustled up the narrow hall at the back of the store where they stowed the mop buckets and the floor buffer, passed by Calvin, who glanced away, turned the corner at Sporting Goods, walked past the row of bikes and tricycles and the stacks of other toys and cut over through House Wares. There were very few customers left in the store at that time of day and most of the clerks and salesmen were hiding out, settling up their day's business so they could get out right at five. Of course he'd be the one to get caught, he the one who had to stay late with some old gal he'd sold before as she tried to decide between the pink lamp or the green one or, worse, which battery to put in her '58 Oldsmobile. Or worse yet something like: "That TV you sold me just won't hold its color. Would you bring it in for me? I'll have to have another one." It was always the blue-headed old women clutching his business card and calling him Mr. Dalrymple that drove him crazy. Still it was a heady feeling being summoned by name. There was a certain fame, a certain celebrity attached to it.

Dalrymple turned into the center aisle, marching as smartly as he could, letting the glow in his eyes out as best he could, putting on the show, preparing his spiel ("When do you want it delivered?" he always began if it was a big-ticket item). Then he saw who was waiting for him. The Old Man, Papa Darnell as he was called among the grunts, Green's district supervisor for the Houston region and

Dalrymple's brother's father-in-law. It was Mr. Darnell who had hired him when he needed a job to support a wife and a new baby, Darnell who had put him in this store because it was hot, Darnell who had saved Dalrymple's neck once and everybody knew he owed him for it. On top of that he was family, so to speak.

"Big Daddy wants you," whispered Buttface Johnson when Dalrymple passed him in the aisle, and Dalrymple whispered back, "Kiss mine, asshole."

He was glad now that he had taken the time to clean his face and straighten up. Appearances were important to Mr. Darnell, and he knew how to do it right. Just look at that suit, Dalrymple thought as he approached: three hundred bucks if it cost a penny and that tie like a flash of fire on his white-shirted chest and that graying hair, meticulously clipped, slicked back for the effect of power, and that little moustache and those black glittering eyes that caught onto you and held tight. He was an imposing figure, a rock, a tower, a benevolent god among mortals.

"Hello there, Dal," said Mr. Darnell, smiling in a sweet, smooth, almost affectionate manner, acting like it had been a hundred years, acting like they were the best of long-lost friends, acting like Clyde Dalrymple, grunt salesman, was something so special in the world that even he, the Old Man, the Numero Uno, the Honcho, was humbled by his presence for a moment and stood in awe. He took the young man's hand in a grip that melted all possible resistance and then pulled him up close to eye him really good, a man-to-man kind of good, and so he could speak right into his face. The handshake never really ended.

"Hello, Mr. Darnell."

At that moment Dalrymple became the center of the universe, the single focus of all his energy. The Old Man had him: eyes linked, hands linked, their businessmen's spirits linked in a kind of secret and somehow sinister brotherhood as if through this handshake they were drawing their trowels from beneath their capes as a signal of secret kinship and holy conspiracy. It was a conspiracy of the old salesman's soul, a kind of bonding, a renewal of ancient and unknown rites, and it drew its power from an overwhelming charisma. Through his cocked eye, the left one, like he was spying through a monocle or a microscope, and through that tight little I'm-something-special smile of his Mr. Darnell exuded this charisma like an aromatic body odor. It was strange, as if he knew things about you that you would never know, never in all your life, and even if you did you would never understand these things as he did. This ritual always baffled Dalrymple, for he had never mastered its finer aspects, its secret, its power, and because of this, along with a peculiar propensity to daydream, Dalrymple knew, as did everybody else, that he was at best a half-assed member of the brotherhood. He always felt uneasy, childish, ignorant in the presence of the Old Man.

"How are you, son?" His breath was a little sour, like a sharp whiff of garlic.

"Fine, Mr. Darnell, just fine." Dalrymple felt himself smiling in a bland hopeful way, wanting to please. "I'm doing fine."

"Good, good, glad to hear it. And your folks?"

"They're fine too, just fine."

"Good. Saw 'em in church last week."

"Yessir."

"But I missed you somehow."

"Couldn't make it, Mr. Darnell. . . . "

He smiled, man to man, Big Daddy to Little Son. And then quickly came The Question: "You selling anything, Dal?"

"Well. . . ." Dalrymple began. Then his face took on the boyish, sheepish look of a loser asking for help. And right off he got it. That smile! Rising up from the Old Man's narrow lips, lifting his blue-veined cheeks, moving into his black eyes, always vaguely amused, which lit up with a father-of-the-earth kind of wisdom, it at once admonished, punished and forgave.

"I know, I know," Mr. Darnell said, shaking it off, and as if by magic a hand rose from a pant's pocket and popped a lozenge into his mouth. "I've seen the report. You're not off by much. It happens to all of us sometimes."

This was a lie, a gift, for It had never happened to the Old Man. He held records from his days on the floor that wouldn't be broken for a millennium; he had tally sheets that Christ himself couldn't match. The prevailing lore held that Darnell could sell the concept of communism to a New Hampshire Republican if there were real money to be made in it.

"I'll do better next month, Mr. Darnell."

"I know you will, Dal, I know you will. I know it. Once we get the hustle back in you."

He suddenly perked up and glanced around the store. He seemed to be looking for something out among the furniture.

"You got a minute, Dal?" he asked without looking back.

"Well sure, Mr. Darnell."

"Good. I'd appreciate a few minutes of your time. I'd like to talk over something with you."

This meant trouble Dalrymple assumed as he followed the Old Man out onto the floor like a dumb-grinning dog on a leash. One of his talks! Nine times out of ten these talks were intended to pep you up, to refire the pilot light, to kick you lovingly in the butt, and when they were over you felt somehow dazed but excited and ever so lucky to be alive and one of the chosen, a prodigal returned and celebrated. It was the ones that were intended to set you straight that could send you home with a dry mouth and a twisted gut. Dalrymple had lived through both kinds: the second kind, a crusher, came on the day back in the spring when the Old Man, a strict believer in Christian norms of behavior, heard about Dalrymple's pending divorce. "Divorce!" he had said. "Divorce! Now you know how we feel about that, Dal. You got to set this straight, Dal, nip it in the bud. Divorce!" the Old Man muttered. He actually held his head over the shame of it, the disgrace, then he laid on the shit with a heavy shovel. It was a lecture full of words such as "morality" and "responsibility" and "uprightness" and "honor" and "humiliation" and "family" and "team spirit" and "righteousness" and even "damnation." And Dalrymple slinked away that evening feeling like a worthless cur, lost and condemned and unworthy. "You rump, you fathead, you loser, you . . . you . . . you fuck-up," he kept calling himself on the way home and then believed it for several days. What could he do to make it right? What could he do? By then it was too late.

Mr. Darnell seemed to be searching for just the right place to settle in that vast prairie of furniture. It was usually a sofa, with him at one end and you at the other, angled toward center so that he had you. He passed up an Early American suite from Basset and a solo contemporary item from Fancy Furnishings and headed for the French provincial—the best in the place, a long boat of a sofa in pale green brocade with touches of mahogany on the arms. It faced the row of refrigerators along the far wall. He took his seat, nodded to Dalrymple to take his, and what a scene: He sat there like it was the most natural thing in the world, as if this were his one true role in life, to be comfortable, to talk, to persuade, to be at his ease. With an arm up on the sofa back, his long legs crossed, a finger reaching out to flick a piece of lint from his trousers, his hand lighting there on his knee, he could have convinced you of anything, anything.

"I got a call today from McCleary," he said. "It was about you, Dal. About this draft business."

"Yessir."

There was a brief silence as the Old Man let this sink in, and Dalrymple could feel the covert looks of his curious colleagues peppering the back of his head. He knew they were out there, finishing up with the last few customers, peeking over lampshades and around the plastic pot plants, sneaking up as close as possible on the chance they might hear something worth repeating. He knew they were doing it because that's what he would have been doing were the victim somebody else.

"Now, you know how we feel about you around here, Dal," said Mr. Darnell, rolling his sleek head over to look at him square. "We see a future, a bright future. You're a smart boy, Dal, and ambitious, I think, I hope. The kind of man we need, Dal."

"Yessir. Thank you."

"And we got plans for you, Dal. You know that don't you?"

Dalrymple almost shook his head but then nodded. And for an

instant his heart lifted with the thought that perhaps Mr. Darnell knew of some way to get him out of this fix too; perhaps he knew somebody on the draft board, or a Congressman or somebody, somebody who would see the absurdity of sending a man like Dalrymple, a man with a future, to a deathtrap like Vietnam. But Mr. Darnell said nothing about that.

"I've figured two years, Dal, three maybe, here on the floor and then a couple of years as an assistant manager somewhere, and then we'd find a store to put you in. As manager, I mean. Your own store. Can you see it, Dal, can you imagine it?"

"Oh, yessir, I sure can. It'd be fine."

"You bet it would. It's what you work for, Dal. It's what all this adds up to. And it's a good life. The money's only part of it. It's the other that's important, the other, you see. The respect from people, the honor of it. They look up to you, you make a difference. It's a responsibility, you see, and we're very careful about who we select. Do you hear me, Dal?"

"Oh, yessir, I sure do."

"I know you do, Dal, I know you do. It's where you belong, Dal, it's where you belong. It's what God intends for you, Dal. I can see it. I know. Do you hear me, Dal? Are you listening?"

"Oh, yessir, I sure do, I sure am."

"I know you do, Dal, I know you do. 'Cause you're a smart boy, Dal, the kind of man we need for the future. We need leaders, Dal, we need men who've been tested by fire, who've shown their mettle, who can hold up to what's ahead, men we can trust. We need captains, Dal, strong men at the bridge. Do you hear me?"

"Yessir."

"Are you listening, Dal?"

"Yessir."

Mr. Darnell nodded his head and went silent for a moment as if caught up in the emotion of his rhetoric, and Dalrymple found himself leaning forward, waiting.

"Now, this business with your wife. . . ."

"Angie."

"That's right. And that little old bit of trouble you had with the police last year—these are unfortunate, very unfortunate, Dal. Drinking and womanizing, Dal, these things can lead to a man's downfall, bring a captain right off his bridge."

"It wasn't me, Mr. Darnell, it was her."

"Yeah well . . . what's the point of nitpicking, Dal? It's the idea of it, the idea of it in a marriage that'll ruin a man, Dal. It's the same with boozing behind the wheel of a car, son, you just don't do it, you see, you just don't."

"Yessir."

"Now, these things were unfortunate, Dal, very unfortunate, but cripes if you can't make your mistakes when you're young, I mean, when can you make 'em. We understand this. We're modern people and we're willing to let it go. It's water under the bridge. It's the past. And now you got to look to the future."

"I sure will, Mr. Darnell."

"I know you will, Dal.

"I sure will—"

"Now, Dal . . . ?" He paused for a long moment.

"Yessir?"

"Dal, I know there's a lot of talk about this war over there—and let's be frank, it's a war—and I know a lot of people are against it. To be perfectly honest I have my own doubts but that's neither here nor there. The thing is, Dal, the thing is, you've been called. Your country needs you, Dal, and it's an honor to serve. You know all of that, I'm not going to go into it, the duty and all that, 'cause you're a good man, Dal, a man who knows his responsibilities. I believe that, Dal. It's unfortunate, I'll hate to lose you by gosh, even for two years, but when the country calls we expect our men to serve."

Dalrymple blinked his eyes and nodded his head.

"It's what we expect, Dal, it's what we expect."

"Yessir."

"Now, Dal . . . ?"

"Yessir?"

"Now, Dal, I know there's a lot of young men, these draft dodgers and card burners and what have you, there's a lot of 'em don't see it that way. They think they're smart, you see. They think there's something wrong with serving, they think they're above it all, they think the communists ought to win this thing. They run off to Canada or some such place and hide out. They abandon their own country in its time of need. I know you know all about it, Dal, and I won't go into it but listen to me, Dal.

"Are you listening?"

"Oh yessir."

"Listen, Dal. Listen. These guys are scum, Dal. They're traitors, they're defectors, they're like spies, that's what they are. You know what I mean? They're just like spies. They ought to be rounded up and shot. Disagreeing's one thing—that's dissent, and it's healthy, I guess, protesting it's called, but you know all that—defecting's another. It's wrong, Dal, it's wrong. It's a crime, it's a sin just like adultery, just like thieving. It's a sin, it's wrong. It leads to hell, Dal, do you hear me?"

"Yessir."

"Are you listening?"

"Yessir."

"Now, Dal . . . ?"

Dalrymple leaned forward to listen. His palms were moist, his armpits, his forehead; his heart beat loudly.

"Now, Dal, I don't want to hear of you getting involved in anything like that. You know what I mean? I don't want to hear of it. 'Cause once you get started it's just like dope, you can't stop. It'll take you over. And the next thing we'll hear is that you're up in Canada living on an iceberg or something, living with the polar bears or the Eskimos."

He tried to grin over his joke.

"Now, Dal, what we got here, down here in Texas . . . well it's like Paradise, you could say. It's like Eden, you could say. The weather, the land, the bounty of the sea, the rich oil under the ground and...and...and the people, Dal, the people by God. The best in the world. It's like Paradise and why anybody would want to leave it, why

. . . well I'll never know. But sometimes we got to, Dal, sometimes the country calls us. Sometimes the troubles of the world are just bigger than we are and more important and they call out, Dal. They call out. 'We need you, Dal,' they say. 'We need you.' And we expect our men to serve, Dal. Do you hear me? Are you listening?"

Dalrymple nodded his head gravely.

"Of course you are, Dal. 'cause you're a smart boy, Dal, a man who knows where his duty lies. I want you to know how proud I am of you, son. And I want you to know something else, Dal. When it's over, when you're out, when you've done your duty, as I know you will, this job'll be waiting for you, this job and then everything else we talked about. We'll welcome you back with open arms. We'll kill the fatted calf. We'll make you a manager, Dal."

The Old Man paused, waiting for something from Dalrymple who, after a long moment, nodded and smiled halfheartedly.

"Don't mention it, Dal."

"Thank you, Mr. Darnell."

The Old Man's pleasant face took on a self-satisfied look, and he sat forward in his seat. It was nearing its conclusion now; he had said what he had to say, it was well after five o'clock and he wanted to be finished, he wanted to be gone.

"When do you leave, Dal?"

"Don't know, Mr. Darnell."

He nodded his head and sat quietly for a moment, deep in thought, the benevolent god spent. He took a deep breath.

"I hope this helped you, Dal. I hope it made things easier for you. We're like a family around here, Dal. We take care of our own and I just wanted you to know that we'll take care of you too when the time comes. You go, you do your job, you come home . . . and then the sky's the limit. You hear me, Dal?"

"Yessir I sure do."

There was another moment of silence, punctuated by a long sigh on both sides, and then without warning the Old Man stood. Dalrymple followed his lead. Mr. Darnell smiled in a fatherly way and put out his hand to be shaken. Again he pulled Dalrymple up close; he draped his arm across the younger man's shoulders, looked right into his face as if to seal a pact and then led him away through the groupings of living room furniture toward the center aisle. The ceiling lights at the back of the store had already been turned out. It was a gray and gloomy place now, full of shadows and uncertainty, though up at the front wall the TVs were still flashing: the evening news now, the forty faces of Walter Cronkite then forty scenes of hot and bloody combat, napalm exploding in thrilling orange balls above the other-worldly green of Vietnam, frightened faces screaming, the chaos and smashed concrete of steamy Saigon, the press conferences at the Pentagon, the release of body counts . . . the same old stuff. It was all so familiar to them by then that it was like a forgotten backdrop on the cafeteria stage from last year's school play.

The office girls were filing out the front, where McCleary had posted himself to lock up behind them, and Mr. Darnell led Dalrymple in that direction. McCleary was waiting. He smiled sadly at Dalrymple and smiled brightly at Mr. Darnell. McCleary and the Old Man exchanged a few words as he was passing out, and then he stopped and turned. He said, "Dal?"

"Yessir?"

"You take care of yourself, son."

"I will, Mr. Darnell."

"I know you will, Dal."

Dalrymple and McCleary waited and watched through the glass as the Old Man paused for a moment on the broad expanse of sidewalk out front of the store. He looked up at the still-hot summer sky, still bright. He looked at the parking lot, a narrow burning shimmering hellish sea of black asphalt and baking automobiles two rows deep. From a pocket he took a pair of sunglasses and put them on and then lifted his gaze to the sky again. He stood perfectly still in the dark shadow of the awning, the only hint of oncoming evening, his hands in his pockets rattling his keys and his change. From the back he looked pensive and kindly and large, a thoughtful man, a conscientious leader burdened with awful responsibilities, one of which he could now put out of his mind. They kept watching as he unlocked his white Lincoln and eased himself inside. Everything he did he did with careful majesty. He backed off from the curb, paused as a Ford pickup passed by and then he put the car in motion. The Lincoln moved through the parking lot with the elegant lumbering grace of a great yacht departing a harbor crowded with lesser craft.

McCleary gave Dalrymple a sideways glance. "Was it rough?"

"Naw. Not too rough," said Dalrymple with a strange kind of vengeful bluster. "What's it matter anyway?"

4.

Dalrymple was living with his parents again at that time, and when he told them about it that evening they showed that absurd kind of parental concern, exaggerated and shocked, which always made him regret telling them anything. They asked him dozens of questions, sought all the particulars, none of which he knew.

"What, you think I work in the defense department or something?" he said. "All's I know is I'm gonna be drafted. Next week, next month, next year, I don't know."

His father kept grabbing his head or shaking it in perplexity and his mother asked, "Can't you get a deferment, Clydie?"

"Ah, Mom! I'm way past that now."

The three of them stared at each other as if the Spirit of Grim Fortune had just swept through the Dalrymple kitchen and touched them all with the spiky finger of mystery. Why us? Why?

Then his mother wept; she took him by the arm and forced him to kneel with her on the kitchen floor for a prayer. On his knees, trying for a little dignity, hoping it wasn't flattening the creases in his pants, Dalrymple stared at the nasty gash in the cupboard door where, years ago during an argument over something he couldn't remember, his father had tried to kick it in. The scar was like a leering smile on the face of an amused god as he watched this little scene. His mother prayed for guidance and deliverance and honor and justice and mercy. She asked what they—they!—had done wrong to deserve this. She prayed for strength and wisdom on the part of her youngest, who hadn't shown much wisdom in his life thus far. It was all embarrassing and Dalrymple later wished his father hadn't been there to see it.

When it was over, once Dalrymple had jumped up and started brushing off his clothes, his father asked just what Ripley had asked: "So, what are you gonna do?"

By then he had at least come up with an answer: "I don't know, just don't know."

"Well listen, don't do anything stupid that you'll regret later, like that business with Angie. Think it through, son."

They gazed at each other in cruel misunderstanding before Dalrymple muttered something under his hot foul smoker's breath that ended with, "What the hell do you know about it?"

His mother said, "Dal, your language."

"Ah, Mom!" But she'd never understand.

"Use your head, son. That's all I'm saying. This is one responsibility you can't shirk. Be a man, now."

It was all so expected! Why had he mentioned it?

He escaped; he went to his room at the front of the house, small like a closet and cluttered with the junk of his childhood and his few manly possessions—a Browning over and under, his collection of pocket knives, the keys to his Camaro, a few magazines and books. He dropped onto his narrow bed to think. In a moment he was up again. He hurried out and down the hall to the bathroom with its faint odor of potpourri and with a good loud gag of relief he deposited his afternoon snack of a Snicker's bar in the toilet. His mother knocked and asked if he was okay.

He said, "Yes fine," and she shuffled away down the hall.

Back in his room he stripped off his sport coat, his light summer slacks, released his neck from the grip of his paisley tie and hung it all neatly on the back of his desk chair. At the front window he looked out and saw his father watering the young pine trees he had recently planted in the yard. He held the hose as he would hold a snake, his thumb over the hole forcing a spray like a silvery fan from the snake's mouth. Still dressed in his suit pants and white shirt, the sleeves rolled up to his elbows, he stood rigid with one foot extended a bit for balance, and he gazed steadily at the base of the slender tree trunk. What was he thinking about? This was a habit of his father, this watering, a ritual, and he did it every evening whether the plants needed it or not. It was a kind of meditation, Dalrymple believed, a putting away of the day, a chance to relax. His father glanced up, saw Dalrymple standing almost naked at the window. He seemed to frown but then glanced away as if he hadn't recognized his own son and didn't want to make eye contact with a stranger. His hair, graying but still thick, caught some of the remaining rays of the sun and glowed sternly for a moment.

"You wish I'd go away, don't you, Dad," said Dalrymple.

He lay on the bed then in nothing but his underwear and socks as the air conditioner hummed in the side window and the gentle evening shadows slowly darkened the room. He had a lot to think about and he was confused. When his mother, standing outside his door, called him for dinner, he called back, without moving, "I'm not hungry." After a moment she shuffled away.

There was always Canada. It was an option, something to think about. Clyde Dalrymple was anything but a radical; he was more an agnostic when it came to the war and to politics in general. He had never burned his draft card, never participated in a protest march, and because his parents were such adamant Republicans, such believers, he even assumed that Richard Nixon was a great statesman. He'd never really thought about it; he'd never voted, wasn't old enough and didn't much care. He was a patriot, sure, a good American, and from his perspective the country just seemed to run itself as if by perpetual motion, as if it were some fabulous machine that would chug along forever with the infinite precision and the breathtaking power and the illimitable sources of renewal of a great and unconquerable star.

It was America, after all, the USofA and if as so many seemed to think it was being threatened by the communists then, sure, somebody ought to go do something about it; they ought to kick some butt. But hell . . . they'd been trying to do something about it for ten ever-loving years already and see where it had gotten them. A mess. A massacre. It was lost.

No. He didn't want to go to the war, he didn't care to fight anybody and he certainly didn't want to die. He didn't want to be a mop in the mopping-up process; he didn't want to be lost in a lost cause. It had nothing to do with courage, he told himself; he was certain of it. He was certain that if he had to go, if he found himself there, in country, carrying a weapon and humping it and fighting for his life, he would comport himself with enough dignity and guts and good sense to avoid at least the horrors of disgrace. It was in his blood; his dad had gone to his war and his Uncle John to his and to hear them talk they were better men for it. But this was different; this was Vietnam; this was a shoddy gray area in the morals of humanity. Isn't that what all those protesters were saying?

No. He didn't want to go, he wouldn't go, he told himself a thousand times in the weeks that followed. He'd be lying in his bed at night, the clock radio whispering beside him, his parents asleep in their room down the hall, or he'd be driving his car on the steamy freeways of Houston, talking to himself out loud as if there were two of him there in the car . . . and it would suddenly come to him: a decision. "I ain't going," he'd mutter to the quiet ceiling of his room or shout to the waiting watching world out there in the city. "Goddamnit I ain't going. By God I got things to do, places to go, people to see. I ain't got time for soldiering, for killing, for dying. I got a future."

School for instance; he was hoping at last to get started that fall at the junior college downtown. Some night courses. Get the basics out of the way before transferring out to the university next year. And there was . . . well just some living to get done too. Now that he and Angie had ripped the blanket he had dreams of fair women and nights on the town. If not this town, if not Houston, then some other town, Toronto or Montreal, such grand cities, he'd heard. They were in Canada, weren't they?

So there was always Canada. But what then? He didn't want to be a Canadian for the rest of his life. He was a Texan, by God, a child of Paradise as Mr. Darnell had put it, and he couldn't fathom the idea of never seeing it again. Of never again seeing the Gulf or hearing its peculiar sluggish roar, of never seeing the Hill Country in springtime with its fields of bluebonnets, never again smelling the sweet, dry desert air out west. And what about his family; what about his son? (Why had they named him Josh? He regretted it now. Why not Sam or Bill or Charlie?) When he grew up what would Josh think of his father, the Canadian?

For days at a time the thought of it never completely left his mind. He had never been to Canada, knew little if anything about the place save the bits of geography and civics any school kid learns. It was up North, way up North, and cold, very cold, and it had a parliamentary form of government, a prime minister instead of a president, or however it worked, and it had those famous Mounties, the fearless men in red, like Dudley Dooright, and it was still owned by the queen of England. Wasn't it? At that time he had never been farther north than Colorado and that was for a one-week vacation during which the five of them—his parents, Dalrymple and his older brother and sister—slept at parks in a rented pop-up trailer and saw the majestic mountain sights. His brother by then was headed off to college in Austin that fall and his sister would soon follow.

They both still lived over there in that bright clean little city with the noble capitol building at its center and all those sparkling suburbs. They were both married now, both slapping together grand careers and healthy families. At least thus it appeared; and his parents reminded him of it as often as possible. His brother was a lawyer, his sister a state senator's aide. Yes. They were successes; they were making their way in the world. He was the last, the baby, he the disappointment: a grunt salesman in a crummy little department store in one of the city's old and fading and almost forgotten neighborhoods.

The Heights.

In the boggy Bayou City, average fifty-two feet above sea level, calling it the Heights wasn't saying much. It was the kind of neighborhood his parents had spent their entire lives getting away from, away from the smell of fried food, the old and listing houses, the insolent men lounging in their undershirts on the sagging front porches, the women's crude shouts up and down the dusty alleys, the dirty children playing on the cracked asphalt of the narrow streets. From such a steaming stew of poverty and deprivation they had risen, and they wanted their get to rise with them, to go beyond. They wanted to forget. But he, Dalrymple, their youngest, their third chance to prove themselves worthy, he, their Clydie, with his paltry job, the people he associated with, his drive each morning across town to The Heights, their son was a sad reminder to them of what they had tried to leave behind, and they despised him for it. He knew; he could see it in their faces when they looked at him, his father especially. Not for the work itself—all work was honorable, they said of course, and he had to work, he had responsibilities—but they despised the intangibles, the sense of failure and the tawdry necessity of his being who he was. And now even his luck had failed him, had failed them all. Again.

Oh Lord, he prayed once that night, the night of the lottery, when fear and uncertainty and disappointment had overwhelmed his thoughts, why can't anything ever go right? In the next breath he said out loud, "I been fucked, man!"

5.

Dalrymple's mother knocked on the door and slipped into his room. She looked like a ghost, her beige chiffon robe hovering above the floor, easing toward him where he lay in his bed. It was well after midnight and he had been lying there awake for hours listening to the whispering radio, a habit that had always served as a kind of salve when trouble caused his soul to fester up. Faintly from down the hall he could hear his father snoring in the instant the door was open. It was like a distant harmonizing echo of the air conditioner's deep gurgling hum.

His mother turned down the radio and sat on the bed beside him. He could barely see her in the glow of the radio's dial but he could smell her quite distinctly: the emphatic woman odors of cold cream and hair spray and lingering perfume mixed with the subtle mother odors of sweat and laundry soap and harsh old worry. He moved under his blankets to make room for her broadened hips. She waited for half a minute, said nothing, settled herself but when she spoke her voice spilled onto him in the darkness, covered him like a shield of reassurance.

"How's my boy?" she said, and he thought he saw her smile. Speckles of light glinted from her eyeglasses.

"Peachy, Mom, just peachy."

She sat for a long time gazing at him helplessly, trying to smile, trying to reassure. And something in the glints of light on her glasses, something in that fluid mother's voice, something in her general presence caused a grave bitterness to well up in his heart, and it made him cold. He shivered in the chill air, and his mother tucked the blanket around his neck.

"Can't sleep?" she said.

He didn't say anything.

"Got a lot on your mind?"

He was silent.

"Oh Clydie," she said. "Why you, h'm?"

"I'm just unlucky, Mom, that's all."

"No you're not."

"Yes I am. Always have been. I'm one of the ones in the world who don't get life on easy terms. That's the best I can figure it. It's probably just as well, I'm doing nothing anyway."

"Don't talk like that, Clydie."

"How should I talk?"

She didn't reply. She sat still and gazed down at him.

His head felt heavy on the old feather pillow, dazed by exhaustion.

Dalrymple said, “What does he say about it?”

“He who?”

“You know who . . . Daddy.”

“Oh.” She was silent for a moment. “Let’s not talk about him just now.”

“In other words he thinks it serves me right.”

“Let’s not talk about him just now.”

They were quiet and just gazed at each other for a while. He saw in her face the lines of middle-age, the pale skin of a woman who never ventured outside a small constrained world. In the glints of light from her glasses, he saw perplexity and sadness.

“Does Mr. Darnell know?” she asked.

“Yes.”

“What did he say?”

“Just what you’d expect. My job’ll be waiting for me when I get back.”

“He’s a good man, Mr. Darnell.”

He didn’t say anything.

“You know, Clydie, you should listen to Mr. Darnell. He’s a man who’s made something of himself. And he obviously likes you.”

“I’m like family, Mom.”

“That’s not all and you know it. You’re a good worker.”

Dalrymple snorted lightly.

“You know, Clydie, we’re not all meant to be big people in the world. It doesn’t mean you can’t have a good life. Some of us weren’t meant to go to college and be lawyers and what have you.”

“You mean like Walter?” he said sarcastically.

“Your brother worked hard to get where he is.”

“I know. And he’s smart.”

“Being smart isn’t everything. If you work hard for Mr. Darnell when you come back you could make a fine career for yourself. A manager of a store . . . or maybe district manager someday. There are people who’d kill for such an opportunity.”

“Ah Mom! that’s not what I want.” His voice was part whine and part cry, full of objection and injury.

"But it may be what you have to take, Clydie," she said firmly, evenly. Then she paused and tried to smile again, and she softened her voice. She touched the blanket, groping for his arm, and when she found it she took it loosely in her grip. "I worry about you, you know. I worry all the time. You're my youngest, you know, my baby . . ."

"Don't, Mother."

"I worry that you're so unsettled and now with this army business . . . you should take what you can get, Clydie."

"What I can get?"

"Don't expect too much, Clydie."

He snorted again and it flustered her.

"Well what do you want?"

"I want to be left alone," he said meanly.

She looked down at him for a long time. He saw no expression in her face, nothing that indicated he had hurt her. Perhaps she expected it, his meanness to her, his sarcasm. Isn't it natural for the offspring to turn on the parent when the real parenting is finished with? What else could she do for him?

"Are you going to school in the fall?" she asked.

"Yes."

She nodded her head. "That's fine," she said. "But you'll have to keep on at the store you know. Your father won't pay for your child support or your car."

"I know."

"He says—"

"I know." His voice had lifted a pitch to stop her and she sat again in silence.

"We all have responsibilities, Clydie, we all have a duty of some kind. I've worked at the same job for twenty years, and your father has been with the gas company thirty years. And you know why? Because we had responsibilities. I pray that Mr. Darnell will understand you and overlook your attitude these days."

"I got nothing against Darnell, Mom, or the store, or any of it, and I know I got responsibilities. But can't you see that I might want more, something else? And why are we talking about this now anyway. It means nothing now. I'm going to the war."

"You were spoiled, Clydie, we all spoiled you. You've made mistakes and you have to pay for them now."

"Thanks for reminding me."

"Be strong, Clydie, for once in your life be strong."

They looked at each other, and in each the other saw a kind of condemnation: it is all your fault as the son who should have listened to my wisdom; no it is all your fault as the mother who raised me so unwisely. Quickly they looked away.

"I'll pray for you," she said, looking back. She reached out then and stroked his hair. In her face he saw a mother's sympathy but nothing that he would have necessarily called love.

"Don't bother," he said.

She slapped him. A light but pitiless slap square against his face. It hadn't hurt him at all but he had seen her hand fly out and had felt it against his cheek as if an insect had blundered into him in the darkness. At first he was shocked—his mother, a weak and docile woman in most concerns, had never before struck out at him—but then he started to smile as one smiles when some great irony has at last revealed itself. He felt the smile wrenching up his face; he couldn't help himself; and in his mind appeared a humorous image of a gnat thinking it could injure an elephant. Her brow was low, her eyes pained, her mouth turned down in an ugly frown of resentment and injury. Her indignation, her constrained fury, made her seem all the weaker to him. He didn't blame her for slapping him; he deserved it; and knowing he deserved it caused the smile on his lips to broaden and deepen, though he knew it would also deepen the wound.

She said nothing. She glared at him. She stood up, still glaring at him in outrageous severity, and left the room. He gazed after her for a long time, long after the door had closed and his heart had calmed to its regular beat.

"I'm sorry, Mama," he said to the darkness.

After a while he turned up the volume on the radio, and once again the distant whispering world entered his room.

6.

Morning, at last. Dalrymple sat on the edge of his bed, smoking, coughing, waiting for his parents to leave. Out there he could hear them: the flush of a toilet, the clank of a spoon against a coffee cup, the closing of a door. At the window he watched his father, dressed for work, starched and creased and polished, checking his fly, walk down the driveway and turn at the street. At the corner, where Merton Lane emptied into Prairie Lea Road, a minor thoroughfare, his father would meet his ride, Mr. Ponce, for the drive into town. A few minutes later his mother backed the Chevy out and drove away. So Dalrymple emerged.

The house was pleasant at that time of day, and he enjoyed being there. It always seemed illicit somehow, his being there alone in the morning. He could do anything, go into any room, any closet, take whatever he wanted.

He had slept very little but in his veins pumped a certain kind of excitement, the exalted feeling that comes from passing through exhaustion to something else, a second wind. He poured himself coffee and sipped it while he took his first piss of the morning. In the kitchen again he poured more coffee and then went out to the little patio at the back of the house. This part of the yard was hidden from the eyes of their neighbors by board fences, hedges of wax leaf ligustrum, the back L of the house.

Sitting in one chair, propping his feet on another, he felt more or less at peace and waited for the steamy day to come on. Birds chirped and flitted among the branches of the trees. There had once been a huge oak tree back here, but to the immense disappointment of his parents it had died several years ago, been taken down, and the young elms, the young willow, the young tallow trees his father had planted in its stead were just beginning to clear the roof of the house. A squirrel was eating at the bird feeder, kicking up seed and making a racket, and a blue jay dove at it from time to time, squawking, trying to run it off.

Dalrymple thought of what he had to do that day. It was a Friday, which meant the big truck would come to the store, which meant he would have something specific and menial to do. He would spend his time unloading hampers of bicycle parts and windshield wipers and paint cans, pricing, restocking. Friday was a good day—he might sell something too, make some money—but he was not inclined to do much. Overnight his mind had linked the store with the government in its crime against him, and he wanted a kind of revenge; it would be the revenge of the lazy and the shiftless, giving as little of himself as he could get away with.

"Let 'em fire me," he said out loud.

He looked forward to seeing Jane that afternoon when she came to work, and he figured he had better go by that evening and see Angie, his ex, to tell her what had happened. Thinking of Angie made his frog of a heart start croaking and brought up the bitterness from his gut—he could taste it—so he turned his thoughts to Jane, Sweet Jane. Jane was a part-time clerk at the store. She was a few years older than Dalrymple, married to a poor pipe fitter and raising a young son, but still they flirted, joked and had even kissed a few times back in the warehouse. *Hey, good-looking,* she had said once in greeting and that's how it started. *Hey, yourself,* he had returned, and they gave each other a look full of that special meaning. For months now the attraction had been deepening, the possibility had been ripening into a certainty until lately it had become apparent that the only remaining questions were When? and Where?

She possessed a large and by all appearances very healthy body and a seething kind of unflaunted sexuality that made Dalrymple burn inside when he got near her. Coupled with this was a shyness, a sweetness, an overripe friendliness about her and a strange vulnerability, almost a sadness. She too had married too young and was stuck now in a resentful union of necessity. Yes. Perhaps today he would make his try . . . what did he have to lose?

Back inside he ate a bowl of cereal at the kitchen table. He read the front page of the *Chronicle* while he ate and paid particular attention to the war news, though the names and developments meant little to him. Then he watched a few minutes of the morning show on television: more war news, a report on the lottery, draft figures, body counts, Nixon in Washington, a plane crash in Idaho. For the first time in his life he was a part of the daily news, he was vaguely famous.

The phone rang as he was stepping into the bathroom for his shower. He didn't really feel like talking to anyone just then, but on the fifth ring he ran into the kitchen and snatched up the receiver. A deep and gravelly but obviously disguised voice said, "Don't go." It was followed by a teasing chortle of a laugh.

"What? Who is this?"

"Don't do it, you little bastard."

The "little bastard" gave him away: "Oh it's you. How you doing, Uncle Blackie?"

Dalrymple heard another laugh on the line that frazzled out into a high wheeze and then a rumbling cough.

"Not too good today," said Blackie. "This heat's awful and my lungs are giving me fits lately, but we're not talking about me just now. Don't you let those sons of bitches drag you off for cannon fodder, son. I got friends in low places, the lowest of places, and we can get you out of this. I promise."

It was good to hear his voice; contained in its hoarse gruff tones was some vague promise of hope in the world, the sense in Dalrymple's heart that somewhere in his own blood was living the inherited chromosome of something like World Knowledge, a different way of living wherein will power and guts led to the potential of getting by even in the realm of harsh reality. Blackie was different from most of them but he was kin.

"How'd you find out?" asked Dalrymple.

"Your sweet mother called, and I read the newspapers, you know. So I thought you might need some advice, and I don't mean the kind your father would give you, bless his Republican's heart. You better listen up while I'm still around to give it."

Blackie wheezed and coughed again, and Dalrymple removed the phone from his ear. It was a painful and frightening sound.

"Hang on a minute," came faintly from the receiver.

Uncle Blackie, Uncle Marvin Dalrymple, the Black Bull, his father's eldest brother, fifteen years senior, had gotten his nickname for legitimate reasons. He was the only one of The Bunch of Nine, as they called themselves, who had ever done anything with his life besides work eight-to-five for a living and raise a houseful of children. The stories Dalrymple had heard about Blackie's life made him out to be nothing but a rascal and ne'er-do-well, and there was at least a whiff of truth to them. But there was more to Blackie, much more, and Dalrymple had always kept a clean closet in his heart for his uncle. He considered himself linked to Blackie somehow through a mystical bonding of the luckless soul. He liked Blackie in the way one fuck-up is drawn to another. And it was mutual: Blackie was the only one of Dalrymple's relatives who had ever given him any special attention. Dalrymple's mother said it was because their birth dates were the same and because Clydie was "the spitting image" of the youthful Blackie. Whenever she spoke of Blackie's youth she did so, Dalrymple knew, by way of warning, an object lesson: "See how Blackie turned out, with nothing but the shirt on his back and a big charming smile. Is that how you want to end your days?" All of which did more to pique Dalrymple's interest than frighten him into submission. He wanted in some hidden part of himself to know all about Blackie and then to imitate, though the courage to do so—to really do it—had not yet materialized in his character.

Blackie's was, to Dalrymple, a wonderful history. In the early years of the Depression Blackie had left school to take a job driving a delivery truck to help the family out and to keep the younger ones at their studies. But he liked to drive too fast, a trait he shared with his young nephew, and one day he sent his truck into a collision with a trolley car on Heights Boulevard. He spent two months in a charity hospital, and when he got out he had a nasty limp and a new attitude. He claimed the company had not properly maintained the delivery trucks and something had gone wrong with the truck that day—the steering or something—and then of course the company left him to the mercy of the fates after his accident. "The lowlifes," as he called all people with money, wouldn't rehire him and did nothing to help him out with his bills. Whatever the truth was, soon after Blackie got out of the hospital he went radical.

He became involved in the union movement, and he got involved in other "shady outfits," as Dalrymple's father put it, and then one day he set out for parts unknown. There was one story that he had been married for a while but Blackie never confirmed this. Other stories had him riding the rails as a hobo, shipping out to sea, working as a lumberjack in the Northwest, all those romantic myths that follow a man such as Blackie. And Blackie never did anything to dispel them. He would show up from time to time during the '40s and '50s, always needing money, always a little more busted up, always a little rowdier and more outspoken and then after hanging around Houston for a few months, maybe a year, he'd disappear again. Blackie would never say where or why.

Then sometime in the early '60s Blackie showed up and stayed, working odd jobs, doing anything to keep himself going. He would arrive for Sunday lunch every few weeks, always wearing his trademark jeans and white sport shirt, and when he sat down at his sister-in-law's prim dining room table, it was as if a bulldozer had come to a grumbling halt in a dainty rose garden. He always dominated such affairs with tales of his adventures, to the great discomfort of Dalrymple's parents, who tolerated him because he was family but considered him an iffy-at-best influence on their three tender children, who generally ignored his stories but found him high excitement nonetheless. After lunch he'd sing songs for the kids, strumming his old guitar inexpertly, or he'd roughhouse with the boys or he'd lend advice as Dalrymple's father finished some project in the garage. And he always helped Dalrymple's mother with the washing of the dishes. Those Sundays usually ended with Blackie snoring away in a restless nap on the den couch and waking up so stiff that he'd have to be helped to his feet by Dalrymple's mother.

Blackie's body was a wreck by then and he soon reached the point where he could barely walk under his own power. Dalrymple's father had been paying most of his bills for several years, though he still earned a little doing handyman work around the seedy apartments he lived in. These "loans" were an awful source of friction among them and his father seldom spoke of Blackie without resentment in his voice. Blackie was rarely invited to the house anymore. Dalrymple had often thought his family wished Blackie would just go away again so they could quit worrying about him and being embarrassed by him. After all, he was a card-carrying Democrat, a union man, a troublemaker.

7.

Dalrymple heard life again on the line. Blackie was sniffling and clearing his throat and muttering about something. Then Dalrymple realized he was speaking to someone else; someone was with him. He heard a woman's voice telling Blackie to take his medicine, and then Blackie snapped at her that he had already taken that medicine and would she leave him alone about it.

She said, "Oh you, what am I gonna do with you."

"Hush now . . . Uh, Clydie, you there?"

"I'm here. Is somebody with you, Uncle Blackie?"

"Well sort of. Yeah. There is. She's a friend of mine. Takes care of me. We go way back."

A hefty feminine voice wailed faintly, "Do we ever!"

"That's good," Dalrymple said and he felt himself smiling.

"Don't tell your folks," Blackie said and the woman giggled.

"No I won't. Of course not." Then: "Why not?"

"Just because, smart ass. You know why. You know how they feel about *love*." He said the word in something resembling a Cajun accent and with a certain inflection as if it were a foreign concept and infinitely humorous. "In fact you know it better'n I do, you and Angie." Blackie laughed his cynical chuckle. "They believe big time in marriage, of course, but they don't necessarily think much of love, especially the carnal kind."

The woman asked in the background: "The what kind?"

"Hush," said Blackie. Then: "She's always butting in."

"What's her name?" asked Dalrymple.

"Her name? Her name?"

Dalrymple heard the feminine giggle again.

"You're gonna like this," Blackie said. "Her name, son, is Georgia T. Ombaugh. She goes by Georgia T. but I myself prefer GTO. And for an old gal her engine still purrs just fine."

"That's quite a name."

"That ain't a name, boy, that's what you call a symbol."

They all laughed.

"Just how old is she?"

"Old enough," said Blackie. "She sure ain't no jail bait. Say maybe you can come by and meet her sometime."

"I'd like to."

"Well do, anytime."

"I will."

"Good. I kind of miss your ugly mug, you little bastard."

For a moment then they were silent, feeling the strange bond again that made of them partners in the business of living and family and staying alive. It made Dalrymple feel better about his uncle's plight knowing he had someone. Dalrymple often worried about Blackie's living alone. He wished he were there now, held close in the warmth of their apparent friendship.

"Anyway. As I was telling you: 'Don't go.' And I mean it. This Vietnam thing, like all wars, son, is just a capitalist plot to gain new markets and they couldn't give a good goddamn about you or me or anybody like us. Don't fight their war, son."

"How am I supposed to get out of it?"

"There're ways."

"What ways?"

"You dumb shit. You should get out more. Canada! Mexico! Try Mexico, and I'll go with you. Hell, son! Fiji for all I know."

"But how?"

"I'm not gonna get into it now and not on the telephone in any case. You know how J. Edgar likes to spy on us all. But when the time comes, we'll talk. When are you supposed to go anyway?"

"Don't know."

"Well don't do anything till you've talked to me."

Blackie went into another coughing fit, and Dalrymple could hear Georgia T. fussing over him.

"Listen, Blackie," Dalrymple said. "I better go. Got to get to work and it sounds like you better take care of that cough."

There was a shuffling of the receiver on the other end, and then the woman came on the line.

"High, honey, it's me, Georgia T., pleased to meet you . . . well, sort of meet you. Would you tell your uncle he ought to go to the hospital, or at least a doctor. He can't get rid of this cough and it's starting to scare me."

The receiver changed hands again, and Blackie said, "To hell with that, I'm fine, just hay fever or something."

"Maybe you ought to listen to her, Blackie."

"And just who's gonna pay for it? Your Old Man?"

"I'll pay for it," Georgia T. said from far away.

"Hush," said Blackie.

"Then I'll pay for it," said Dalrymple.

"Get real, kid. You keep your money. You're gonna need it for passage on the Underground Railroad."

"The what?"

Blackie laughed. "Dumber 'n dog shit, this one. You little bastard. Listen. We'll talk. You come see me. Okay?"

There was a long silence before Blackie said softly, "Look, Clydie, try not to worry. You're a young man, have some fun for Christ's sake. Get out. Meet some women. Hell fuck some women. Don't sit around and mope over this."

"No I won't."

"You okay, son?"

There was another long silence. Dalrymple longed again to be with Blackie and Georgia T. there in Blackie's apartment with its shabby curtains and its used furniture from the Goodwill store and its smell of neglect and tobacco and night sweats. He longed to hide in the shelter of his uncle's hard experience and protective knowledge. He felt hot tears coming into his eyes but couldn't have said where they had come from or why. He almost said *I love you, Blackie* but his uncle would not have understood this and he would have teased him without mercy. No that's not it: He would understand, but he would brush past it with hard teasing nonetheless; this was the way of the men in the Dalrymple clan.

"Listen, Blackie, I . . . I better go," said Dalrymple in a voice that even he could tell was less than convincing.

"Keeping the lowlife's time are you," Blackie said in his blustery tone. He knew, he did understand, there was no point in saying it out loud. "Well everybody's got to eat, I guess. But you listen to me: don't you do anything till you've seen me and we've talked. You hear me, you little bastard?"

"I hear you."

"All right then. Take care of your old self.

"I will . . . you old bastard."

"Hah!" snorted Blackie. "That's the way."

He chuckled and coughed for a moment, huffed out, "All right then," and the line went dead.

"Blackie?"

Nothing. That's how he always ended a conversation: it just stopped. Dalrymple stood there a moment thinking about his uncle and what he had said. He wanted to listen to his uncle, he hoped he had an answer but there was something about Blackie that always frightened Dalrymple. He felt his uncle wanted him to do things he wasn't sure he could do. In everything between them there was a sense of challenge, the challenge to prove himself masculine in all the rougher meanings of that word. Blackie was the kind of man who could get you into big trouble. Still, speaking to Blackie had lifted his spirits, and he went into the bathroom whistling a lighthearted tune.

It felt especially good to shower and shave that morning. He thought he had finally washed off what had happened to him the day before. He dressed casually, in comfortable loafers and old slacks and an old sport coat. He turned off each of the three air conditioners in the house and then locked up.

His car, the Camaro, was parked at the curb. He started it and just listened for a moment as he lit up his first cigarette for the drive to the store. He enjoyed the deep growl of the Camaro's V-8, the whooshing intake of its four-barrel carburetor, the faint clatter of all those valves. He kept it immaculate, inside and out, because he liked driving a clean car and he liked to show it off. Besides the child support he paid to Angie each month, the car was his primary obligation in life. The payments were more than he could afford, but he felt it was important to have something in life, something that was truly yours, something worth working for. He would miss his car.

It was time to go. He put the car in gear, popped the clutch and laid rubber for twenty yards as he sped down the street. He'd probably hear about that later (the neighbors would report), but he grinned all the way to the freeway.

8.

That day Dalrymple floated. A bit lightheaded, he was like a bubble of foam above the shocking ocean breakers of crude living.

The morning passed with blessed speed. It was busy at the store. About nine o'clock the company truck arrived and stock boys started rolling canvas hampers through the warehouse and onto the floor to be unloaded. They banged through the big brown doors at the back and rumbled like bumper cars all over the showroom. Then a truck from Old Colonial showed up with two sets of new living room furniture and all the salesmen gathered to comment. "Ugly as my first wife," said one of the old guys, and they all laughed, throwing out other cruel but accurate observations. Huge and overstuffed, the sofa was a cheap boxcar covered in the tackiest possible floral print, dull brown on dull beige, and no one could figure out what kind of flowers were being depicted. Dalrymple said nothing; he wasn't sure they would have even listened. His colleagues seemed to be trying to ignore him, or avoid him, as if he were a ghost now or a dying man.

Which was fine with him; they meant nothing to him, and he would not miss them at all.

While all of this was going on Dalrymple quietly sold a double-door refrigerator, a console television-stereo combination and a set of top-of-the-line Super Forty tires, the last to a man with a Camaro similar to his own. In just a few hours, as he figured it, he had made enough commission to pay half of his child support for the month—a good day—and it had all just walked in the door looking for him. He'd had to do nothing but write up the sales. So he decided to take it easy for the rest of the day, just get through until five o'clock.

When he came back from lunch Jane was in the store. He sensed her presence before he even saw her across the showroom talking to McCleary back near the bedroom furniture. McCleary was smiling, leering ludicrously, joking with her. All the men, even good old McCleary, ogled her and tried to get close. Dalrymple figured he was giving her instructions on what to do for the day, a two-minute task that he could always stretch into fifteen.

Gee-god! she looked good, especially from a distance. Her hair was thick, pale like winter oak leaves and pulled back from her face, which had no sharp angles, no disturbing lines, though the general appearance of that face was one of heaviness, thickness, like that of a very handsome draft horse. There was something rough about her as if the human sculptor had lost interest in her before finishing the task of creation. She was dressed in a black jersey with a red rose painted on the front in such a way that the stem angled up between her breasts and the flower lay against her collarbone. But it was the lower half that made men stare: those great strong big-woman thighs covered by the skimpiest of red mini-skirts. It sent an ache through his loins just thinking about what was so thinly hidden up underneath that hem which cut across her pale skin a good hand or more above her knees. What made it all the more appealing was that it seemed she had no idea she was so appealing. To her it was just the current fashion, the kind of stuff you bought at K-Mart for ten bucks or less. It was cheap and she knew it, everybody knew it.

Suddenly McCleary pointed at something up front, and she followed where he pointed. Then she saw Dalrymple. He could tell in the way her face at first brightened and then darkened when she realized that someone might have noticed the attention she threw out to him so casually. She immediately dipped her chin out of shyness, acting as if she were listening to McCleary. But she couldn't help herself; she waved. McCleary looked up, grinned when he saw who she had waved at.

They met at the time clock at the back of the store, smiled at each other without speaking, and then punched in. It was 1:11.

"Hey, good-looking."

"Hey yourself."

They looked at each other and knew, knew it was coming, and soon. He would try it today, somehow, something, at least set the thing in motion. He felt he was looking good, he felt the fire of manhood in his veins after his talk with his Uncle Blackie and his successful morning. To hell with the others who were already sending him off. He wasn't gone yet; he was still here, still a functioning go-getter. Money, or even the prospect of it, made a man attractive to women, he thought; they could smell it on you; they could smell the success like a subtle aftershave. He had the sense of her sniffing around him for the signal scent and now he had nothing to lose.

"I heard," she said, frowning.

"Heard what?" he said.

"You know, the lottery."

"Oh that."

"It's so unfair, this war! What are you gonna do?"

So it was this, the sense of the tragic about him, that made her eager and interested, even loving. Success meant nothing to her. He thought for a moment and said, "What I'd *like* to do is get a peek at what you're hiding up under that skirt." Then he blushed. He felt it spread up from his neck and across his face all the way to his scalp. She blushed too and playfully tapped his shoulder with her fingers.

She smiled through the blush and said, to Dalrymple's astonishment, "Well I'd like to show you."

It had been building to this for weeks.

Just then somebody walked by and they separated, walked away, watching each other through the shelves of merchandise as they hurried toward Automotive up parallel aisles still crowded with hampers. It was a kind of game with them, racing through the narrow aisles, tossing out taunts of "I'm gonna beat" or "last one's a rotten egg," and it often made their faces flush like the faces of children at play. When they got to the checkout counter, a customer was waiting with a can of upholstery cleaner in his flabby hand. He was a fat man with a midsection like an inner tube and a thick coal-black beard that lacked a moustache and gave him the appearance of a New England minister from the last century. He regarded them severely. Dalrymple and Jane glanced at each other and grinned, almost laughed out loud, and then made an effort to comport themselves with the dignity appropriate to employees of Green's Furniture and Auto. While Jane busied herself with a hamper, Dalrymple rang up the man's sale and sent him on his way with a "you come back now." Then he bent and looked between two shelves of car-washing sponges and tins of polish, and he said to Jane, "When?"

"Whenever," she came back lightly and blushed again, smirked with embarrassment, glanced away.

"How's about right now?"

"Can't now, silly."

He made a fake and exaggerated frown and turned away to the counter where the big cash register squatted like a sculptured God of Money. He punched the button for his drawer and then the NO SALE button. His cash drawer clattered out, tapping his thighs, and he removed his nametag. She came around the long shelf holding a boxed headlight in her hand, and she leaned against the counter, not a foot away from him, eyeing him closely with a sweet little twist to her plain lips. She wore no makeup at all—didn't really need it and probably couldn't afford it.

He fumbled trying to pin his name tag to his lapel, so she put down the headlight and helped him. Their eyes met briefly, and they smiled again. Dalrymple glanced around. It was that time of day when the employees were in and out for lunch and only a few customers in the store and sure enough there was no one close-by just then, no one who could see. Quickly, in a burst of enthusiasm and unwonted courage, he thrust his hand under her skirt and cupped her crotch with his palm. She did nothing but look at him with that faint and appealing twist in her lips, though he thought perhaps she spread her thighs just enough to let his hand get the whole effect. What he felt was firm and full and warm, and her underpants were moist. Soon she became shy again and glanced around herself, and then suddenly she backed away as if someone were coming. No one was; it was just the jitters, and it made everything all the more exciting.

"Satisfied?" she said hoarsely.

"No."

He had a horrible, painful erection, covered by his trousers and his jacket, but she knew. She stepped up to him again and gripped it firmly in her hand and gave it a quick shake, and when she let go he saw that her face was bright red and her eyes were shining. A little bubble of spittle appeared at the corner of her lips. His own mouth had gone dry and he blinked at her.

"Someone's coming," she said.

They separated again, went to different hampers and started pulling out the new merchandise to price and put on the shelves. A middle-aged woman in a business suit walked up to the counter. "May I get some help please?" she said, and Dalrymple straightened, put his hand in his pocket to cover the bulge in his pants.

"Yes ma'am," he said loudly. "What can I do for you?"

"I need a battery for my car. And I'm in a hurry."

Glancing back at Jane with only a half-hidden smile, Dalrymple led the woman to the display of batteries and went into his spiel. While he told her about the various batteries, trying to sell her up to the Super Sixty, he could hear Jane working her hand-held pricing machine—*ka-thunk ka-thunk ka-thunk*—and the sound of it, the regular rhythm perhaps or the thought of her hands manipulating the machine, made him want her more than ever.

His customer bought a battery but then changed her mind once he had written it up; she'd take the Super Sixty after all. Then he was told of some problem with one of his deliveries, and he had to deal with setting up a new time. Other interruptions followed (he sold another television and a dinette table) and it wasn't until 3:30 or so that things calmed down. Most of the hampers had been unloaded and removed to the warehouse, the stock boys were either gone for the day or out helping on the delivery trucks, the other salesmen were busy with customers or writing up delivery orders, and a kind of hush fell upon the place. The old building itself seemed to let out a long deep and settling sigh before the last push to closing time.

9.

Dalrymple was standing alone up in Appliances, taking a smoke break, catching his breath, staring at but not watching a soap opera on the televisions when Jane scurried up, brushed passed him, said over her shoulder, "Meet you in the warehouse," and then scooted away, wagging her butt outrageously. This meant she had checked. The warehouse was empty of people. She threw him a look then and he knew what it meant. Then she waved a long gray dust rag at him as if it were an alluring hanky.

He had almost forgotten about her in the commotion of the afternoon but now, excited by all his activity and the money he had made and feeling generally good about his day, the old eagerness resurfaced and quickly agitated his loins. He dropped his cigarette to the floor and stepped on it with the heel of his shoe. Then he meandered his way through the Furniture side of the store to the back. Before pushing through the doors he hesitated, looked for observers, but no one was paying any attention.

The warehouse was long and narrow, a two-story rectangle. It was quiet now. Even the downstairs area, where earlier there had been so much bustling about, was sullen and mysterious and echoed with his footfalls. Dalrymple crept up the wide wooden stairs to the second floor, lighted by only a few naked bulbs. It was up there that they stowed the leftover Christmas merchandise and the new bicycles and the mattresses by the dozens in their large brown boxes. The place was a study in gloomy shadows, with many dark and hidden places, everything coated in gritty dust and dotted with mouse shit. He turned a corner and then another and found her waiting for him back in their usual corner. She playfully waved the dust rag again and tried her best to look inviting. And she did look inviting: those long legs and arms showing, that neck, all that hair. His heart was a croaking frog in his chest, and he felt the excitement sounding through his veins.

They said nothing. There was nothing to say. They kissed once, a long dry one, but he could taste the health in her like candy on his tongue. She responded, the dust rag still in her hand, waving about his head and shoulders, and then they were smearing each other with kisses. Dalrymple's hand found her crotch again and groped. She was moist again.

What happened then came to him as if in a dream, as if he had only imagined their mingled breaths and mingles limbs and mingled scents. Her skirt came up, her underpants went down—he actually shoved them to the floor with his shoe without even looking so that she could step one foot out—and somehow his fly was open and she had him in her hands. Then he was pushing inside her. It had been so long! and he had the feeling of experiencing something new in the world. Their breathing came like the snorts of a locomotive, and his shoes kept slipping on the dusty wooden floor. And then she eased herself back into the V between two slanting mattress boxes and he was almost on top of her. She kept whispering, "Oh Dal yes, yes," and when he looked once he saw that her eyes were closed in an impossible and unexpected ecstasy. He glanced around to see if anyone was coming, but she quickly drew him to her again. He tried not to think about what he was doing; it was so incredible; he just took what was being offered. "Hurry, Dal, hurry," she whispered and he felt himself falling into a strange and glorious place. He groaned once and settled against her and after a moment more it was over.

"Oh Dal, finally," she said. "You were full and ready weren't you." They rested quietly, breathing into each other's ears but trying to listen for intruders and every second seemed an hour long. "You're a fine lover, Dal," she whispered.

"Shhh."

He winced at the term—lover?—and wondered at her ignorance and realized in an instant that perhaps this was the only kind of love she had ever known: hot and quick and dirty. Giving only and never taking or demanding her own woman's pleasure. Already he wanted to get away from her.

Lemons! No. Lemon oil. The pungent odor struck his nose and seemed to fill his head. He could even taste it. And then he felt something against his neck and realized it was her dust rag draped across his shoulder. He realized that she had never let go of the thing. and wondered if the oil in the rag was staining his jacket or his shirt collar; in the same instant his stomach gave a lurch and he felt the revulsion pump up through his body. It was as if she had vomited in his hands; and he despised her.

Dalrymple stood up, arranged himself, zipped and put out a hand to her. It was Dalrymple who bent down and pulled up her underpants. He saw then that they were red like her skirt.

"You okay?" he said, suddenly feeling brutal.

She only nodded and smiled. He saw a streak of dust on her cheek and reached up to brush it away. Their fingers met, and she took his hand in hers and held it to her face.

"I wish it could have been more, Dal, better somehow."

"It was fine," he said and nodded his encouragement and his thanks to her several times. They looked at each other with such uncertainty that it was apparent she couldn't believe what had just happened either. Why had she done it?

"I've never done anything like this before," she said.

It was a lie obvious enough but understandable.

"Me either," he said.

"Maybe next time—"

"Shhh."

They blinked at each other and tried to smile, and then it came to them both that they had to hurry.

"Listen," he said. "You better go first."

She nodded again and then kissed him on the cheek. She smirked in embarrassment as she had done earlier at the checkout counter, an annoying tic to him now, and she moved away from him. Before turning the corner she looked back and offered a quick smile. She waved the dust rag once more in playful farewell and was gone, clumping down the stairs. He heard the big doors open and then wheeze shut and he was alone.

Dalrymple lingered in the silent warehouse and smoked a cigarette and tried not to think about what this meant. But it was impossible. He could still smell the lemon oil and his own body odors heightened by his exertions, and he could smell her odors too. Mingled with the dry itchy odor of the dust it all seemed perverse and disgusting. Again he felt the brutality of what he had done and thought himself loathsome, but he felt also that she had wanted and expected it to be just as it had been. He tried to imagine what in her simplicity she would expect of him now. Had he created another responsibility, another problem? He paced, smoking, pleased with himself but worrying all the same.

Then he heard his name called over the loud speaker.

"Oh shit! Gee-god! You idiot! You louse! You fuck-up!"

It sounded at first like the voice of God condemning him for his depravity. He froze, listening, feeling caught, frightened and uncertain what to do but to linger would only heighten his apparent guilt. So he rushed down and out into the bright showroom where he was certain everyone would be looking at him, waiting for an explanation. By the time he reached the main sales counter, sort of a corral at the center of the store within which worked the office girls and the manager, he realized that none of them suspected a thing, none of them had even missed him.

Waiting for him was a pair of customers, an elderly black couple with whom he'd been dealing for months. They liked Dalrymple. The man was a municipal employee in the Parks Department, and they had been putting away money for years to furnish their little house one last time before retirement. They were ready now to do the living room. Didn't take long. By 5:30 Dalrymple had sold them one of the two sets of the Old Colonial stuff that had arrived in the store just that morning along with tables and lamps and even a rug. An eighteen-hundred dollar sale.

The news spread all through the store.

"I just love it," the old woman said, her soft body jiggling with excitement in its print dress. "And brand new you say."

"Yes ma'am, it's something all right," Dalrymple said.

As he was writing it up he glanced over and saw Jane grinning at him from across the corral. She was even proud of him, as if he were her son or her husband. He quickly looked away and tried to ignore her, afraid someone would notice. Soon, along with most of the other employees, she filed out the front of the darkened store and disappeared into the sweltering afternoon to meet her husband in his Plymouth. He felt at last set free.

"So when do you want it delivered?" he asked the couple.

They agreed on Monday. They all shook hands and he showed them to the front, joking with them and reassuring them in a salesman's easy encouraging terms that they had made the right decision. McCleary had stayed behind until Dalrymple was ready. They left together. As they were parting for their separate cars McCleary said, "Damn, Dal, you had a pretty good day."

Dalrymple couldn't disagree.

"By the way, when you gonna get you some of that Jane gal?" McCleary asked, winking with ludicrous familiarity. "It sure looks like she's got something for you in a big way."

"She's married," he said.

"That's the best kind, my friend. Experience! And you can smell it all over her. She ain't getting enough at home. Do her a favor, Dal, and then tell me all about it."

Dalrymple felt himself blush, and for a moment he considered telling McCleary his Jane-in-the-Warehouse story but such boasting would certainly get around. He liked Jane. He kept quiet.

"You okay, Dal?" asked McCleary.

"Yeah thanks," he said.

"Say listen, try not to worry too much about this draft shit. Maybe something'll come up. You never know."

They yanked off their ties and jackets and got into their cars, like heated ovens, and McCleary waved before he drove away.

"Goddamn!" Dalrymple screamed joyfully in the car.

He felt good and it was good to be in the Camaro again, once the A/C had cooled it down. He flew through the narrow streets of the neighborhood, racing the engine at intersections, grinning challenges at the other drivers who looked over. He was nineteen and strong, he was healthy and handsome, he'd just gotten a little and made a lot of money; it was summertime, lush and green and full of the promise of summery things—he had the urge to kick off his shoes and drive barefoot—and maybe life wasn't such a mean old nasty bugger after all. The army, the war, the menacing world in general seemed very far away, off there in the future, a vague shadow in his thoughts now and a lot could happen between now and the future. All the way to Angie's house he kept shouting, "You genius! you lover! you hotshot!" and he hummed snippets of old songs while he waited in traffic on the steaming freeways of the great and sprawling city.

10.

Angie was not in the best of moods. For one thing he should have let her know he was coming; she had a date that night. And for another she needed a car; she needed his car.

"Oh great," she said when he appeared at her door. "I just don't have time for this. What a day."

She turned and went to the kitchen leaving him to come in or go away as he saw fit. His nose told him it was dinnertime.

The house was small, two bedrooms, a box with windows in one of those Baby Boomer neighborhoods that had flourished in the city's southwest quadrant in the '50s and '60s. It sat at the dead end of a street of similar little houses, each one needing paint and yard work, each one obscured to some extent by old cars and pickups parked at the curbs and even an eighteen-wheeler in one case. Just the kind of neighborhood he couldn't fathom himself living in now. There was no cul-de-sac; the street just ended at a low weedy berm littered with paper debris and broken bottles, and on the other side of a twisted and listing chain-link fence ran a Southern Pacific railroad line. Twice a day the walls and floors of the house rumbled and shook as if in an earthquake when freight trains sped by. They had rented the house in the last few months of their marriage, and Dalrymple had liked the place back then, despite the noisy trains. It was homey and had a large yard in back where he had at first planned, in those days when he was trying his best to be a grown-up family man, to do all those things people with houses do to make them even homier. A hammock he had hung was still out there stretched between two rangy elms, the only trees in the yard. Everything else had that sad neglected look of a house in which a death has recently occurred. The grass was knee-high in places; the old flowerbeds were choked by weeds and the dead stalks of long-gone plants; and toys lay all around like discarded and forgotten bits of brightly colored happiness. Looking upon it all brought to his mind again the chaos of their life together, from beginning to end, for in those two years there had never been any real peace or beauty or sense or permanence. Nothing about it had been tended properly, nothing nurtured, and the weeds of discontent had at last won out.

Dalrymple closed the door and followed Angie into the kitchen, a box within a box. It housed a chrome-legged dinette table and aged appliances in a harvest gold color. The window above the sink looked out on the ugly and dilapidated vacant house next door, about twenty feet away, which was supposed to be haunted by the ghost of a suicide victim. Which meant the owner had a hell of a time renting the place, for the neighborhood children—of which, Dalrymple had estimated, there must have been about a million—always made a point of coming around on their bicycles to shout this fact to prospective tenants whenever the man showed the house. Whether it was the ghost or the children who made the people hesitant to rent Dalrymple had never figured out.

"Well it's good to see you too," he said at the kitchen.

She looked over from the stove and said, "How many times do I have to tell you? Call first."

"I forgot. And it was a busy day."

"Tell me about it."

"What's wrong with you?" he asked, but she didn't answer.

He stood in the doorway and stared at her. She was a good-looking woman, not in the way of Jane whose robust body seemed to be always about to burst out of its clothing whether she intended it to or not but in a thinner, smaller, more subdued and more demure way. From a distance she looked rather like the very young wife of an executive or a businessman or perhaps she could be a college coed. She had just then a kind of rusty-blonde dye in her hair, which she liked to pile up on her head. Her skin was smooth and milky-colored, and her small breasts rode high on her body as if always on the look-out for something. Which she was. Her sharp narrow face, so often severe, could be sweet at times.

"Where's Josh?"

"My parents, for the weekend," she said as she stirred something in a saucepan on the stove. "Mama came and got him."

That meant more than likely she was planning on a weekend guest of the male variety. The house inside was neat and tidy, he had noticed. She worked a short day on Friday and so, he assumed, she had spent her time doing housework, perhaps another reason for her foul humor since she hated cleaning anything but herself. She worked at a boutique, Darla's Hanger, which sold expensive clothes to rich women over in the Galleria area. With her discount at the shop she dressed well in Darla's clothes. Just then she was wearing a pair of too-tight jeans of some fancy design and an outlandish Western shirt with sequins all over it, the tail tied up at her waist. Her feet were bare. And little drops of perspiration dotted her narrow upper lip.

"Boy, the yard's a real mess," he said.

"Don't start on me, please."

"I wasn't starting anything," he said and wondered then why in hell he had come here. He had no idea what he was looking for, what he expected from her. Always with her in the back of his mind, and even now, was the possibility that if he saw her something would click or fuse between them and thus spark a renewal of the old emotions. This was unlikely, especially today, but still in many regards she was his closest friend since his old high school buddies had mostly abandoned him during the time of his marriage, drifting away, leaving for college. Because he and Angie were connected in other more intimate ways he had thought she should know that something awful and life-changing had happened to him. He had planned to come and so he came and now he regretted it.

He said, "You want me to come by and mow on Sunday?"

"No," she said. "My brother will do it next week."

"Oh."

She looked at him and mocked, "Oh," in a fake-masculine voice. They gazed at each and almost smiled.

"What do you want anyway?" she asked.

"Nothing. I'll tell you later."

"Better be quick. I'm in a hurry, sort of."

"Got a date?" He smiled without wanting to.

It was like a switch had been turned in her mind by an obscure sense of guilt. She looked at him with more interest and even an air of kindness. It was false; she wanted something; but it was better than being tolerated as a familiar intrusion.

"Actually," she said sweetly. "It's kind of good you're here. I need to talk to you about something."

"What's that?"

"Oh just something. Have you eaten dinner?"

"No. And that sure smells good."

"It's just noodles but as long as you're here you may as well eat. I never meant for you to go hungry. Sit down."

At the sink she drained the noodles through a colander and then went back to the stove. From the cupboard she took a jar and handed it to him at the table.

"Open that for me would ya? It's store boughten but I kind of like that brand of sauce."

She took it from him, turned and dumped the contents of the jar into the saucepan with the noodles. She went back to stirring. It was one thing about Angie: she never had been and never would be much of a cook. Eating to her was just something you did to keep from being hungry and she much preferred to do it out. He watched her; there was something endearing in her efforts and something appealing in her movements. Her body churned and wiggled as she worked the spoon, the left hand on her hip, and when she paused her lips pouted and her eyes went serious. From time to time she would glance over and smile at him self-consciously.

Dalrymple lit up a cigarette, and she immediately began to fan the air behind her with her free hand as if shooing away flies that were bothering her butt.

"We have a new rule around here: no smoking."

"I don't live by rules with you."

"Since when?"

"Since you know when."

"Well there's one rule you're gonna have to learn to live by real soon," she said.

"What's that?"

"Just a minute."

She took down two plates and two jelly jars and put them on the table. Then she clattered around in a drawer and came up with two mismatched sets of silverware and dropped them on the table in a heap. Next appeared a loaf of white bread, a tub of margarine and a couple of paper towels. She bustled about with great purpose in her movements and a faint, distant but very handsome frown on her face, which meant she was concentrating.

"I think it's ready," she said.

From the saucepan she spooned out two large portions of the spaghetti stuff and stood there looking pleased with herself.

"I call this Spaghetti Stuff," she said brightly and smiled. "Let's see, what else. Oh! The wine."

"Wine? Where'd you get wine?"

"Roy."

Neither of them was old enough to buy liquor but she had always been good at nurturing associates who could. She poured out two full glasses and finally sat down.

"Well here's to you," she said and took a long sip, her left hand pressed against her chest as if to steady herself. She set her glass down, put on a serious face and said, "It's just this simple, Dal: I need the car."

"What car you talking about?" he said with a full mouth.

"Your car."

"My car!" he said and a bit of sauce flew out of his mouth.

"It was part of our deal, Dal, as you know perfectly well."

"What's wrong with your car?"

"Ka-poot," she said. "Something in the engine. I had to have it towed home. Daddy's gonna see what he can do to sell it for scrap." She shook her head sadly and said, "That poor old VW."

"But Angie I got to have my car for work."

"Me too."

"But I can't afford two cars."

"You'll just have to figure out some way to do it. I can't be left without reliable transportation. Think of Josh. What if I had to rush him to the hospital or the dentist or something."

"The dentist?"

"You never know. He's growing up, Dal."

"How would you know? You don't see him any more than I do. He's always at the day care or your mother's."

"Let's keep this conversation on a civil level, please. There's no reason to shout."

"I ain't shouting," he shouted and remembered then that one of her complaints against him had been his hot temper. He had been trying to improve this aspect of his character ever since the divorce. So he tried to calm himself as they glared at each other over their plates of Spaghetti Stuff.

They both heard it coming. The evening train. A faraway whistle. And the sinister rumbling of the floor and then the walls as it came closer and the tremendous noise and power of it intensified. Soon it was on them, the overwhelming thunder and the steady clicking of the wheels, and they waited in a tense and distressing silence. To speak then would have meant to yell, and they knew better than to try. They both ate a little and waited, glancing up, sitting there like animals caught in a cage during a great storm. Angie shrugged once in apology for the interruption. Then it had passed. The thunder and the shuddering of the tiny house subsided and they heard again the faraway whistle, and they both took deep breaths of relief. But it was as if the passing of the train had taken away their energy to talk anymore and they sat there with their own thoughts for a long time.

"Your supper's getting cold," she said at last.

Dalrymple had lost his appetite. His wonderful afternoon had been ruined. The thought of her getting his car stabbed into his heart with the dismal and mysterious force of despair. She was right though: it had been part of their separation agreement that he would see to it she had "reliable transportation for a period of no less than three years" following the divorce. It had been understood by all that this meant the Camaro if she needed it. He had always thought Volkswagens ran forever, but then Angie had never had any idea how to tend to a car. She had probably let it run out of oil and burnt up the pistons, something stupid.

"I'm sorry, Dal," she said, her voice softer. "I know what that car means to you. I'm not doing this just to be mean. I've been worrying about it for two days, I've been sick over it. But I'm a woman with a child—your son, remember—and I have to be independent. Think of me, Dal."

He got up quickly and paced a few steps in the narrow kitchen. It was all so familiar; they had had numerous such awkward and at times angry discussions about possessions and arrangements and love and even fidelity in the final months of their marriage. Somehow they always ended in the kitchen where he paced and cursed while she sat at the table and watched him.

He said he'd need some time. She said she could give him a week; Darla could pick her up and drop her off for that long. She said again she was sorry. He said being sorry didn't count for much. She said, "I know that."

Dalrymple stood at the sink and looked through the window at the vacant house next door that was supposed to be haunted by the ghost of a suicide victim. He tried to think of a way out of this, but all he came up with was a heavy feeling, the terrible weight of responsibility that rose from the lingering thought that he had ruined Angie's life when he got her pregnant and still owed her for it, despite her transgressions. He wished he had never come here. All he wanted to do was leave.

"Aren't you gonna finish your supper?"

"I gotta go," he said and hurried from the kitchen.

"Wait a minute," she called. "Didn't you have something to tell me?"

"Never mind," he said. "It's not important."

"Dal, wait," she called again. He heard her chair scrape against the floor, and then she was standing in the kitchen doorway, leaning against the doorjamb. She seemed sad to see him leaving. Her face was sad, full of regret and uncertainty.

"You know, Dal, this has nothing to do with love. I still love you. I guess I'll always love you, in some way, after what we went through together. I just don't want to be married to you, that's all. That's all it is."

"Oh. Well that's good to hear," he said sarcastically, and she smirked to show that she understood the sarcasm and perhaps even understood the absurdity of what she had said. They looked at each other for a long moment before he stepped through the door and into the suffocating heat of a Houston evening.

At the carport he raised the hood of the VW. Several engine parts were lying there loose in the well, and a number of important wires dangled free like the rigid tentacles of a dead sea creature. Obviously the mechanic had just given up on it. He slammed the hood and kicked the chrome bumper and once again he saw doom in everything that pertained to his life. He sat in the Camaro for a long while, thinking he'd lay rubber and make a big defiant noise in leaving, but it would just give her cause to laugh at him, yet another mean victory over him. A belch rose from his aggrieved stomach, and he tasted the Spaghetti Stuff again. He let out the clutch and drove away quietly.

11.

In the back of the place, boxed in by a little alcove, two construction workers were playing pool quite peaceably. They seemed to be friends and even friendly, their white teeth flashing smiles from time to time. There was only one pool table in Dick's Dive Inn, and its green field, illuminated by a hanging beer sign showing off waterfalls on two sides, glowed with such intensity in the otherwise dark interior that it reminded Dalrymple of a ball diamond as seen from high up in the stands during a night game. The men were scruffy and large, dressed in jeans and tee shirts and heavy boots, and both of them wore gimme caps low above their eyes like the shades of card dealers so that their faces were always in shadow. Down their backs dangled ponytails. As one of them bent over the table, the other stood watching, back in a corner, the cue stick held before him propped on the floor like a lance, and he sipped his beer as he waited to shoot.

That's what Dalrymple wanted: some companionship, friendly conversation over a game of pool. But more than that he wanted a beer, several beers if possible. That's why he was here. After seeing Angie he had driven around for a while trying to decide what to do with himself or to think of someplace to go, sulking about this latest development with Angie and his car until he got depressed and thirsty. He didn't much feel like going home to spend the evening with his parents watching television in that eerie personal silence that always sprang up between them these days when they had to pass time together. Especially now, after what had happened; it would cause so much new tension that all the old disappointments and misunderstanding would simmer up until the silence between them would become unbearable, a tangible discomfort. Such evenings made Dalrymple feel like they were three travelers waiting in a bus terminal, strangers thrown together out of luckless necessity who felt obliged to make conversation while they waited to depart in different directions. It was a kind of non-conversation; it was just extra noise above the noise of the television; talk for the sake of talking.

No. He didn't want to go home. It was Friday night after all and on Friday nights a young man ought to be out on the town. Dalrymple saw this as something kin to the migrating of the birds; a natural urge that rose up in him by instinct and long habit from his high-school days, that halcyon time of football games and movie dates that ended early and abruptly for him when Angie got pregnant. He often felt, and some who knew him would have agreed, that all he had gotten from high school was this habitual and powerful urge to be out carousing on Friday nights.

Dalrymple didn't know quite what was expected of him here in Dick's Dive Inn. He had been in a bar only once and that was with McCleary who handled everything with expertise. McCleary had ordered the beers at the bar and brought them to the table and joked with the barmaid and treated Dalrymple as if he were an old drinking buddy who simply didn't care to leave the table. Dalrymple got so drunk that it embarrassed and worried McCleary, and he had never offered to do it again. So now he was on his own.

And there was also the age thing. What if they carded him?

He could see the barmaid at the bar, talking with a customer. She had glanced around when he came in but didn't seem to be in any kind of a hurry to serve him.

He had chosen a table close to the door in a dark corner, thinking he might appear twenty-one or better if the barmaid couldn't see his face very well. He had worn his jacket and drawn up his tie in the hope that his appearance would make him look like a businessman who just happened to stop in this joint for a quick beer on the way home. He noticed that of the eight or ten people in the place he was the only one wearing a tie. Frankly he dreaded the initial contact. If she asked for identification he had no idea what he would say, and he hated more than anything to be embarrassed in public. He had chosen Dick's, located at the end of a seedy little strip center a few blocks from Angie's house, because he had seen it many times when he used to stop for milk and bread at the 7-11 on the other end of the shopping center. The storefront glass had been blackened and Dick's Dive Inn had been inexpertly painted on the glass in crooked white letters. He thought perhaps it was the kind of place that just wouldn't care if he was of legal age to drink.

Dalrymple lit a cigarette and looked around. Dick's was grimy and small and dark, lit up here and there by a dozen or so beer signs on the walls. There were perhaps ten tables, mostly empty. The two men playing pool had racked the balls and were preparing to start another game. At the bar sat three men, each one hunched over, serious drinkers. At one table sat two men in blue work uniforms hotly discussing the Astros' chances of success. At another sat a middle-aged couple whispering.

All of a sudden the barmaid was standing at his table. She was a chunky gal of about thirty-five wearing outlandish pink hot pants and a white ruffled blouse, loosely buttoned at the top to reveal the upper orbs of an enormous pair of breasts. Her hair was dark and stringy, clipped at the shoulders. A great deal of hard living showed through her made-up face, and on the lower lid of her left eye glowed the lingering blue-black crescent of a bruise. He assumed it had been caused by a punch in the face. She put down a napkin on the table, smiled so warmly at Dalrymple that for a moment he thought perhaps they knew each other, perhaps she had seen him around, and she prepared to take his order.

"What'll it be, my friend?"

She cocked her head to one side, brightened her eyes and smiled again with such friendliness that his heart pumped wonderful relief all through his body. No problem, he thought.

"A beer," he said.

"Okidoke. What kind?"

"Uh. What have you got?"

She seemed startled by the question but said, "You name it we probably got it."

"How's about a Schlitz."

"We got Schlitz, sure. A Schlitz it is then. Bottle or can?"

"Uh. Bottle, I guess."

"Okidoke. A bottle of Schlitz." She gazed at him as if sizing him up for something, but she still offered him such a friendly, almost motherly face to look upon that he wasn't prepared for what she said: "You're so handsome and young-looking, I'll declare, that I'm afraid I'll need to see some kind of I.D. We've had the state liquor boys in here lately. They've tried to close us down once and we don't want 'em to try it again."

He knew the "handsome" bit was a line with her, a politeness that she reserved for such occasions so as not to embarrass away tips. And she seemed like the type who wanted to give you what you wanted, who wanted to cause trouble for no one, who couldn't have cared less about the law when it came to a trivial bottle of beer because she had had a hard life and knew that so much of living was a marginal thing. It was in her eyes, her ugly battered face: enjoy and relax and cause me no trouble and I'll do what I can for you. But it was her job; it was expected of her.

He felt hot blood rise into his face, and he thought of what he had prepared to say about having lost his driver's license and having no other kind of card on him just then, and he imagined in the same instant that she would change. He saw her ugly battered friendly face going stern and unfriendly with disbelief and derision and self-importance; he saw her turning to the room and shouting something about a deadbeat trying to get over on her. To lie to her would do him no good at all. So he floundered about for something to tell her, and what he said came to him without rehearsal and as a complete surprise:

"Look, ma'am, I found out yesterday I'm gonna be drafted soon . . . and'll probably go to the war . . . and it's been a hard day . . . .and, you know, all I want is a beer."

Her face displayed no emotion, nothing.

"Couldn't you get me a beer?"

It took a moment more and even then the smile rose on her pudgy lips so slowly that at first he wasn't sure it was a smile. But then it formed, and she held it steady as she gazed down at him with her experienced eyes. It was a sweet smile, an accepting smile, a smile that said well at least you didn't try to pull one on me, you didn't lie to me as so many have. Her eyes blinked several times, and this caused him to notice again the nasty blue-black bruise that brought up his sympathy and his contempt and it made of her a woman repellent and appealing all at once. A black eye? What could this nice woman possibly have done to cause a man to throw his fist into her face? Such a friendly face.

She put a hand on the table and leaned against it. She looked at him again in that searching way as if to see for certain that he was telling her the truth. And he saw again that pity which so many had shown him in the past two days.

"I'm sorry—"

"All's I want's a beer. Just a beer."

"I'm sorry but . . . drafted?"

"Yes."

"You've been drafted?"

"Yes. Or will be."

She shook her head in contemplation of the thing. She frowned, thinking about it, and raked back her hair.

"You'd think that if I'm old enough to go to the war that I ought to be old enough to drink a beer. Wouldn't you?"

She shook her head again and looked at him as if he had told her something outrageous, which nonetheless touched something inside of her. She smirked noisily and glanced back at the bar as if to see if the bartender were watching. Dalrymple looked too and saw that the man was busy washing glasses.

"Just a beer," Dalrymple cajoled.

"My little brother died in that war," she said.

Suddenly her face changed, went mean and hard and bitter, and she looked at him as if he were the cause of the bitterness. For a moment she seemed transported in her thoughts to someplace far away and dangerous. Then she changed again, and she blinked and looked at him and her eyes spoke of pity and disgust and outrage as if she hated him for reminding her of something she had tried to forget. "A beer huh?" she said. "That's what you want?"

He nodded. She turned and marched away through the tables to the bar. She handed a bill to the bartender who took it and quickly produced a bottle. He opened it and set it on the wood and after saying something to him she took up the bottle and hurried back through the tables. When she arrived she hesitated for a moment, standing above Dalrymple with the beer in her hand, looking down at him, showing that hard bitterness in her eyes again. With no preliminaries she sat down in the chair across from him. She leaned up close to the table as if to whisper so that her breasts flattened against the wood.

"This is my beer," she said. "But you can have some, you see. Drink it real fast and then get out of here."

This was nothing like what he had expected. It was more like a punishment than a reward.

"Look," he said. "Let's just forget it."

"No go on, drink it."

He took a sip. She glanced over her shoulder to see if anyone was watching. Her face was completely cold when it returned to him. "Gimme some of that," she said. She took the bottle and turned it up, drank half of it and set it down in front of him. "So you're gonna be a soldier are you?"

"Looks like."

She nodded thoughtfully and said, "My old man was over there too. Someplace called Khesanh. 1968." She shook her head and raked back her hair. "Lost an eye," she said, lightly touching her right cheek by way of emphasis. "Made him mean, real mean."

"Yeah, I can see that."

A world-weary kind of cruelty entered her face when she looked at him now, and he thought for a moment she was going to say *you don't know shit* or stand up and tell him to get out. It was a long bad moment, and he wished he hadn't said it, wished he hadn't noticed the badge of suffering under her eye nor acknowledged that he knew what it meant.

She said, "Drink up."

He took a sip and then handed her the bottle. She finished it off and put a hand against her chest when she belched.

"So you want beer tonight, is that what it is?"

"Yes."

"You want to get drunk, is that what it is?"

He shrugged and almost smiled.

"You think that's what soldiers do?"

"I don't know what soldiers do, yet."

She shook her head and rolled her eyes away in a look of such complete derision that Dalrymple felt like a fool. Without warning she said, "Come with me," and then stood up. She raked back her hair and challenged him with her eyes. "Well come on."

"Where to?" he asked.

"Just come on."

He followed her out the door and into the evening where the summertime heat flooded over them, almost pushed them back inside with its oppressive force. The sun had just set and the western sky was a rage of hot color though the sidewalk under its awning sulked in a deep shadow. He towered above her pudgy body and saw for the first time a thin spot in her dark hair at the crown of her head. She said, "Come on." She walked quickly up the sidewalk, and he followed like a child in trouble. They passed several empty storefronts, saying nothing, until they had almost reached the 7-11. She stopped and turned to him and said, "Gimme five bucks." She held out her hand and urged him to hurry.

He dug into his pocket and fished out a bill and gave it to her. "Wait here," she commanded and then marched off again, pushing through the door. A few minutes later she emerged from the store with a brown bag under her arm and approached him.

"Where's your car?"

He nodded toward the Camaro.

"Come on," she said.

Together they walked to the car. It was in the far, darkening corner of the lot. Cars and trucks pounded by in a pack on the street after the light at the corner changed and all around them, up and down the ragged dirty street, neon signs had begun to flicker on. Exhaust fumes fouled the air and everything was dirty, littered with debris and broken glass.

"Get in," she said, speaking up over the traffic noise.

Again he obeyed her without comment or question. He unlocked and opened the door but then stood there before sitting down.

"Go on, get in," she said.

He did. She closed the door and then tapped on the window for him to roll it down. She leaned on her elbows against the door and looked in at him, her face so close that he could smell the powerful odors of her unwashed hair and her barmaid's hard working body and even the beer on her breath.

"Start it up," she said.

He turned the key, and the Camaro growled to life.

"Well done. You're a good little soldier. You'll do fine."

She hefted the bag up and handed it in through the window. He took it from her and set it down on the seat beside him.

"Nice car," she said flatly. "Still smells new inside."

He smiled and nodded.

"There're two six packs in there," she said. "That ought to be enough to get you drunk, soldier boy."

"Listen," said Dalrymple, finding his voice. "My name's— "

"No don't tell me. I don't want to know."

She stood up straight and looked down at him. She smiled in her old friendly way. A dismissive and indulgent and half-sad warmth came into her ugly battered face again, and for an instant he thought she might reach out to touch his arm. So that what she said surprised him. "You're nothing special, you know."

He just looked at her. Her black eye flashed.

"Nobody owes you nothing," she said.

"I know that."

"Nothing! You hear me?"

A van passing by on the street let out a honk, and she flinched as if she'd been struck by a bullet. She changed again; she was through with him. Her face was hard and brutal. She bent low and leaned in the window so he would hear what she said clearly. Her ugliness by then was so complete and profound and threatening that he recoiled and tried to pull away from her.

"Now get out of here, you little fuck head, and don't come back again."

He wiped her spittle from his cheek and with a strange sinking feeling deep in his stomach he watched her walk away across the scabby parking lot. The door to Dick's Dive Inn opened and then closed behind her. She never glanced back.

12.

He had no place to go so he just drove around for hours that night, drinking beers, warm beers after the first two, remembering that barmaid's face and voice and her bewildering attitude. She seemed all at once tender and hateful toward him.

He drove the freeways mostly, all over the city, slipping down into familiar neighborhoods from time to time to get out of the light and the noise and the rush of traffic. Once, about midnight, he drove back by Angie's place, saw the red Pontiac parked out front that must have been Roy's and in a stupid rage he tossed his five empties onto her lawn; then he laid rubber.

At home he hid the second six pack in the trunk of the Camaro, crept into the house, banged into a floor lamp that his mother had recently moved in a rearrangement of furniture and then into his bedroom. He slept soundly.

Early the next morning, just before waking in a sweat, hung over slightly from the beer she had purchased for him, Dalrymple dreamed of that barmaid. It was a fearful dream that would plague him all through the months of July and August that year and into the autumn; through the winter too and into spring, though with less regularity, it would not let his mind alone and even in the month of May 1972 as he lay for the first time on a military cot in a warm open and metallic-smelling army barracks at Fort Polk, Louisiana, amid the night-bug sounds and the harsh erratic snoring of some two-dozen comrades—one of whom screamed "Mama!" rousing half the new-boy-men-soldiers on the second floor with his nightmare—it always drove him, Private Dalrymple, when he realized it was The Dream, to flee the awful spectacle, to force himself from sleep.

It began with the sensation of heavy breathing. As if he had been running for a long time and had to keep on running. As if something were chasing him. She was there, just ahead. They were in a gentle lovely place, a seemingly endless forest with tall trees above them and soft green ferns on the ground and dappled sunlight all about. He had been following her for some time, trying to catch up to her, always about to call out "Wait, wait!" when quite suddenly she stopped and turned. She was dressed in crimson lace with a crimson bow in her hair, and she was holding out her pudgy hands to him. He wanted to rush into her arms and be held but the sight of her stopped him. It was a moment of horror and uncertainty for on her face appeared long fresh scars like razor cuts and huge puffy bruises like putrid plums and her lips were bleeding over a smile of enticing beauty.

About the Author

Paul Scott Malone has published stories in many of the leading fiction journals and anthologies. His first collection of short stories, *In An Arid Land*, won the prestigious Jesse Jones Award for Fiction from the Texas Institute of Letters. Mr. Malone earned the MFA from the University of Arizona and now writes full-time. A former Texan, he currently lives in Illinois.